A RING OF ROSES

BY

JOHN BLACKBURN

with a new introduction by
ADRIAN SCHOBER

VALANCOURT BOOKS

A Ring of Roses by John Blackburn
First published London: Jonathan Cape, 1965
First Valancourt Books edition 2014

Copyright © 1965 by John Blackburn
Introduction © 2014 by Adrian Schober

Published by Valancourt Books, Richmond, Virginia
http://www.valancourtbooks.com

ISBN 978-1-941147-34-4 (*trade paperback*)

Cover photograph © Shutterstock.com
Cover design by M. S. Corley

Set in Dante MT

A RING OF ROSES

JOHN BLACKBURN was born in 1923 in the village of Corbridge, England, the second son of a clergyman. Blackburn attended Haileybury College near London beginning in 1937, but his education was interrupted by the onset of World War II; the shadow of the war, and that of Nazi Germany, would later play a role in many of his works. He served as a radio officer during the war in the Mercantile Marine from 1942 to 1945, and resumed his education afterwards at Durham University, earning his bachelor's degree in 1949. Blackburn taught for several years after that, first in London and then in Berlin, and married Joan Mary Clift in 1950. Returning to London in 1952, he took over the management of Red Lion Books.

It was there that Blackburn began writing, and the immediate success in 1958 of his first novel, *A Scent of New-Mown Hay*, led him to take up a career as a writer full time. He and his wife also maintained an antiquarian bookstore, a secondary occupation that would inform some of his work, including the bibliomystery *Blue Octavo* (1963). *A Scent of New-Mown Hay* typified the approach that would come to characterize Blackburn's twenty-eight novels, which defied easy categorization in their unique and compelling mixture of the genres of science fiction, horror, mystery, and thriller. Many of Blackburn's best novels came in the late 1960s and early 1970s, with a string of successes that included the classics *A Ring of Roses* (1965), *Children of the Night* (1966), *Nothing but the Night* (1968; adapted for a 1973 film starring Christopher Lee and Peter Cushing), *Devil Daddy* (1972) and *Our Lady of Pain* (1974). Somewhat unusually for a popular horror writer, Blackburn's novels were not only successful with the reading public but also won widespread critical acclaim: the *Times Literary Supplement* declared him 'today's master of horror', while the *Penguin Encyclopedia of Horror and the Supernatural* regarded him as 'certainly the best British novelist in his field' and the *St James Guide to Crime & Mystery Writers* called him 'one of England's best practicing novelists in the tradition of the thriller novel'.

By the time Blackburn published his final novel in 1985, much of his work was already out of print, an inexplicable neglect that continued until Valancourt began republishing his novels in 2013. John Blackburn died in 1993.

By John Blackburn

A Scent of New-Mown Hay (1958)★

A Sour Apple Tree (1958)

Broken Boy (1959)★

Dead Man Running (1960)

The Gaunt Woman (1962)

Blue Octavo (1963)★

Colonel Bogus (1964)

The Winds of Midnight (1964)

A Ring of Roses (1965)★

Children of the Night (1966)★

The Flame and the Wind (1967)★

Nothing but the Night (1968)★

The Young Man from Lima (1968)

Bury Him Darkly (1969)★

Blow the House Down (1970)

The Household Traitors (1971)★

Devil Daddy (1972)★

For Fear of Little Men (1972)

Deep Among the Dead Men (1973)

Our Lady of Pain (1974)★

Mister Brown's Bodies (1975)

The Face of the Lion (1976)★

The Cyclops Goblet (1977)★

Dead Man's Handle (1978)

The Sins of the Father (1979)

A Beastly Business (1982)★

The Book of the Dead (1984)

The Bad Penny (1985)★

★ Available or forthcoming from Valancourt Books

INTRODUCTION*

In John Blackburn's 1965 novel, *A Ring of Roses* (published in the US as *A Wreath of Roses*), English schoolboy Billy Fenwick mysteriously disappears from a train passing through East German territory. Amid speculation that he has been the victim of a political kidnapping or tragic accident, he reappears days later in West Berlin. His distraught parents are relieved to find him back in England, safe and well, it seems – until he succumbs to illness, with a temperature over 107. A general practitioner, Jackson ('Jacko'), is called in to treat the nine-year-old. But, worried and unsure about his diagnosis, he asks his esteemed bacteriologist friend Sir Marcus Levin, KCB, FRS, for a second opinion. As the good doctor cautiously forms his diagnoses, Billy's disease-ridden body is medicalised, read as a text for signs and meanings:

> He opened Billy's pyjama jacket and as he did so he stiffened. No, he thought, it's not possible. You're jumping to conclusions like 'Jacko,' because it's your own subject. The child has never been out of Europe – it can't be possible. He pulled out a lens and studied the spots. They were rather beautiful: a ring of dark red roses sprinkled on the pale skin [. . .]
>
> He ran his hand over the child's body, over the flat belly, past the tiny, underdeveloped genitals and into the crotch, searching for the thing that he dreaded to find: the hall-mark which belonged to the greatest killer in history. It was there all right, just as he knew it would be, hard and throbbing under his fingers, and he could almost feel it growing. Almost as large as a walnut now, soon it would reach the size of a small orange and then burst. When it did so Billy Fenwick would probably be dead. (46)

---

* PUBLISHER'S NOTE: As the introduction contains a detailed discussion of the novel's plot and reveals several of its twists, readers unfamiliar with *A Ring of Roses* may wish to read the story first and return to the introduction afterwards.

In the fourteenth century the Black Death had swept through Europe and killed around half of its population. It was indeed 'the greatest killer in history'. And so when Sir Marcus declares a national emergency, it's a race against time to trace Billy's contacts and prevent this modern outbreak of *bacillus pestis*, or bubonic plague, whereby the past threatens to wreak havoc on the present, with potentially devastating consequences for humanity. But is this plague a regenerative mutation, a freak of nature, a man-made disease? The work of a highly secret state-sponsored biological warfare program or an individual? As per Blackburn's method, you can take your pick of red herrings. Overcoming mutual suspicion and mistrust, East and West Germany, with their respective systems of alliances, must work together to eradicate the biological threat, or else it will be a plague on both their countries. Crucial assistance is provided by Sir Marcus, in the first of several teamings with General Charles Kirk of the British Foreign Office Intelligence Service. But here Kirk takes a backseat to Marcus.

In setting most of his novel against a divided Germany, Blackburn was clearly tapping into Cold War tensions and anxieties, à la John Le Carré or Len Deighton. His novel came out just four years after the Berlin Wall was erected by the German Democratic Republic – i.e. Soviet-aligned East Germany – to stem the flow of people emigrating or 'defecting' into the more affluent, fast-growing Western sectors. The Wall thus became a potent symbol of oppression and desperation behind the Iron Curtain. On August 17, 1962, the world was shocked when eighteen-year-old Peter Fechter was shot by border guards while attempting to climb over the Wall into West Berlin; he bled to death on the East Berlin side for about an hour without medical aid. When President John F. Kennedy, on a visit to West Berlin, June 26, 1963, made his potentially incendiary 'Ich Bin Ein Berliner' speech, he was not only voicing American support for the city and 'universal' principles of freedom, but condemning Communist policy. Although Blackburn eschews social commentary, he conveys something of the desperation and hopelessness of East Germans at the time. Granted, he draws readers into Billy's nightmarish vision of the train journey, the child's mounting terror as he listens to the freedom seekers attempting to enter his sleeping compartment when the train comes to a halt: 'He pulled the blankets tightly up to his chin and tried not to scream, though he knew that at any moment the window would come down and he would see a hand slide in under the blind. The tapping stopped, there was another deep laugh and he could picture fingers fumbling for the window catch' (4). But as General Kirk summarises the plight of East Germans for Billy's parents (and, of course, readers), since the building of the Wall only a very few are able to flee, using the secret escape routes to the West: 'tunnels under the Spree River, basements extended into the Allied sectors, ways through the sewers and the disused railway tunnels where the barriers have been removed' (37). These escape routes, which figure importantly in the plot – not least as a route of transmission for the plague – are run by a highly organised resistance/escape-helper network.

That the threat in Blackburn's novel is bacteriological rather than nuclear coincides with extensive research and development into biological or germ warfare in the UK, US and the former USSR during the war and postwar eras. Spurred on by unreliable intelligence that the Germans were developing biological weapons during the Second World War, the UK embarked on a highly classified germ warfare program at its Porton Down research facility, Wiltshire, once mentioned in the novel. In 1942, they tested anthrax bombs on sheep at Gruinard Island, Scotland, and as part of Operation Vegetarian they mass produced 'cattle cakes' containing anthrax spores, as a counter to German biological attack. To help mass produce these bombs, the UK called on their US ally who, in the following year, set up their own facility at Camp Detrick (later Fort) in Frederick, Maryland. As it turns out, none of these biological weapons were used during the Second World War. However, after the war, the US program became larger still, as did the Soviet Union's, while the UK gave up its offensive research in the mid-1950s. In 1972, the signing of the Biological Weapons Convention treaty by the US, Soviet Union and other countries was a formal renunciation of biological weapons, now deemed unlawful. In fact, the Soviet Union was continuing to enlarge its program (under its secret bio-warfare agency, Biopreparat), the full nature and extent of which only came out with the collapse of the regime.[1] Thus, in hindsight, the vacillations and suspicions of Marcus, Kirk and Gregor Petrov of the MVD that the pestilence has been hatched in a biological weapons laboratory from the other side of the Iron Curtain, was not unreasonable and more within the realm of science fact than fiction. Certainly both the Western Powers and Soviet Union had the scientific means and intent and both had every reason to be suspicious of what the other was doing. And, while the suggestion that both sides will come together for the common good may seem hopeful, even naïve, to some readers, Blackburn at least offers a more nuanced view of the Cold War that grants our Communist 'adversaries' a certain humanity. As Kirk soberly puts it: 'Adversity makes strange bedfellows, as they say, and our friends behind the Iron Curtain don't want an epidemic of plague any more than we do' (50).

In the wake of revelations and leaks about research and development into biological weapons, stories about the desperate efforts of medical and other authorities to prevent or control the spread of deadly diseases became more common in the Cold War era, particularly in the US. These stories represent a particular type of medical thriller, wedded to the disaster story. For instance, in Charles Eric Maine's *The Darkest of Nights* (1962, UK) the medical community prove ineffectual in containing the global spread of an unknown virus, which has possibly been mutated by nuclear explosions. As the scientific, administrative and executive elite retreat underground, the remaining populace degenerate into riots and insurrection. Harry Harrison's *Plague from Space* (1965, US) chronicles efforts to control the spread of a disease which has been tailor-made by an extraterrestrial intelligence, while in Michael Crichton's *The Andromeda Strain* (1969, US) an extraterrestrial virus owes its outbreak to a US bio-warfare program. Of the disaster story, *The Encyclopedia of Science Fiction* notes that 'Oddly enough, where UK writers reveal an obsession with the weather, US writers show a strong concern for disease.'[2] For the record, the novel which launched Blackburn's career, *A Scent of New-Mown Hay* (1958), contains both elements, and has Kirk and UK research biologists doing all they can to curtail a weird fungoid mutation which absorbs the human tissue of its female victims without killing them. The titular new-mown hay refers to the smell of the fungus which is carried by the wind. And setting the precedent for later Blackburn novels is 'the Nazi connection': sociopathic German scientist and war criminal Rosa Steinberg, who has unleashed the fungus as retribution for Germany's defeat by the Allies. In *A Ring of Roses*, Frau Doktor Trude of the SS medical research centre at Dachau turns out to be a red herring. Interestingly, in neither this novel nor Blackburn's earlier treatment of the plague theme are Russians responsible, but instead a mad scientist.

As in *Children of the Night* (1966), *Bury Him Darkly* (1969) and other Blackburn works, *A Ring of Roses* concerns the very Gothic threat of the return, the return of the Black Death. When Marcus considers the ring of truth to the nursery rhyme, 'A Ring of Roses', traditionally attributed to the plague, it hardly matters that this interpretation of the rhyme has since been discredited. For, by now, Blackburn has merged fact with fiction. As Marcus speculates on Billy's movements at the time of his disappearance, he sifts through his reference library on plague, and pulls out a translation of Vogel's *The Great Pandemic of the Middle Ages*. He looks up the German town of Rudisheim associated with the outbreak of the plague and in particular the beliefs and superstitions attached to the fourteenth-century abbot of a Benedictine monastery, one Rudolph von Ginter, who was sentenced to death by the town. According to the legend, the monastery became an accursed place after his death, haunted by the figure of the Black Virgin or Plague Maiden who rode on the shoulders of a corpse. When a Lutheran church was much later established on the site, a bronze casting of the mad abbot's head, believed to be his death mask, was found and kept in the church, where it remained until the end of the Second World War, when it mysteriously disappeared. Despite the questionable nature of this account, Marcus follows a hunch which takes him to Rudisheim and the site of the church/former monastery. There he meets wannabe priest-cum-scientist, Karl Arnim, who still lives with his *mutti* (in an Oedipal relationship that would possibly make Freud cringe!) Naturally, the megalomaniac Karl is responsible for unleashing the plague onto an unsuspecting world

– when he opened the life mask of von Ginter and found that it was carrying still-live spores of the bubonic bacillus, he set out to develop a more virulent strain in rats. We learn that he deliberately infected Billy with the original strain, whilst in the care of Arnim's mother, a resistance worker with the Brothers Grimm codename Clever Gretel. Unwittingly, Karl infects himself with the new strain (ironically, one of his own rats bites him). The palm-sweating climax has the 'dying, rotting' Karl making his way through the sewers and disused underground railway that comes out into West Berlin's British sector to find others to accept his lethal 'legacy' (141), while authorities work frantically to locate him and destroy the disease at its source.

A Ring of Roses shows how Blackburn was not above recycling his own ideas and plots, and he would return to the theme of disease in The Young Man from Lima (1968), Devil Daddy (1972), The Face of the Lion (1976) and A Beastly Business (1982). Yet, in my opinion, A Ring of Roses is one of his very best thrillers. Not surprisingly, it was positively received by critics. 'Lively action plus the genuine frissons inherent in any good account of epidemiology',[3] opined Anthony Boucher of The New York Times; while Peter Vansittart of The Spectator thought it an 'efficient, quick-moving tale'.[4] For Kirkus Reviews it was 'a professional handling and, on the whole, lively deadly stuff',[5] but the Times Literary Supplement had the most praise: 'John Blackburn is our only current writer who can induce such terror as the Grimm brothers did, and some of the Grimm characters are among the ingredients in this hellbrew of the return of the Black Death.'[6] Though the diverting plot may rely a little too heavily on Marcus's hunches, Blackburn paints an authentic picture of post-war Berlin (where, in the early 1950s, he lived with his wife and worked as a schoolteacher for the Control Commission, under the Allied occupation). There is also just the right balance of scientific exposition and action, and, with his crisp, polished prose, Blackburn was one of the most stylish popular writers of his generation. As with several of his other works, A Ring of Roses was optioned for a movie that was never made, and only Nothing but the Night (1968; filmed 1972) has made the transfer to the cinema screen, with middling results. But, if done right, *A Ring of Roses* would make an exciting, suspenseful movie.

Adrian Schober
April 23, 2014

Adrian Schober has a Ph.D. in English from Monash University, Australia, and is the author of *Possessed Child Narratives in Literature and Film: Contrary States* (Palgrave Macmillan, 2004). He has published in a range of journals on literature and film and his essay, 'Welfare, Motherhood and the Best Interests of the Lost/Possessed Child: John Blackburn's *Nothing but the Night*', has appeared in *The Journal of Popular Culture*.

NOTES

1   Jeanne Guillemin, *Biological Weapons: From the Invention of State-Sponsored Programs to Contemporary Bioterrorism* (New York: Columbia University Press, 2005).

2   John Clute and Peter Nicholls, eds., *The Encyclopedia of Science Fiction*, accessed February 21, 2014, http://www.sf-encyclopedia.com/entry/disaster.

3   Anthony Boucher, 'Criminals at Large', *The New York Times*, November 7, 1965, p. 84.

4   Peter Vansittart, 'Groves of Academe', *The Spectator*, August 6, 1965, p. 185.

5   *Kirkus Reviews*, October 15, 1965, accessed March 21, 2014, https://www.kirkusreviews.com/book-reviews/john-blackburn/a-wreath-of-roses-2.

6   'Crime in Short', *Times Literary Supplement*, September 2, 1965, p. 760.

A RING OF ROSES

One

In the distance he heard the locomotive whistle and the train clanked slowly across what sounded like an iron bridge and ground to a halt. It was the sixth stop since they had left Berlin.

Billy Fenwick lay very stiffly in his upper berth of the sleeping compartment and he knew that it was the sixth stop because he'd counted every one of them. He also knew that the time was exactly twenty-five minutes to two and that they should be almost half way to the border by now. The wrist watch which he'd strapped to the rail of the bunk was a treasured possession, given to him on his ninth birthday, and every other minute he glanced at its luminous dial. Anything to pass the time, to stop him falling asleep, to keep him from staring at the window blind which, in the blue light cast by the little bulb over the door, looked like a sheet of shiny metal.

But he shouldn't be frightened because he was nine years old now. A great, big boy, as they kept telling him. Mummy had promised him that there were no monsters outside and it was just his imagination. Robin wasn't frightened and he was only five and a half. Billy leaned over the bunk and looked down at his brother, who was curled up fast asleep with his head buried in the pillow which had 'Bundesbahn' embroidered across it in red silk. He looked so still that he might have been dead.

No, Robin wasn't frightened, but why should he be? Robin was too young to know why the blinds were pulled down so tightly. He couldn't picture the cold desert outside with its coils of rusting barbed wire and the tallow-faced people who stood and watched the trains. Robin didn't realize that at every stop there was danger, that at this very moment the people were coming towards them and, if the train didn't start again soon, one of them might raise his hand, open the window and begin to climb in. Billy stared across at the blind again. In the dim light he couldn't read the message which was written across it, but he knew what it said all right. 'Allied personnel are ordered not to raise the blinds while the train is passing

3

through East German territory.' Daddy had told him that was because of something called a security agreement, but he knew better. It was because of the grey people who were waiting in the cold.

And two of them were there now. A dribble of sweat ran down his forehead as he listened. Yes, footsteps were coming across the tracks, somebody was speaking in a low guttural voice, somebody laughed, and there was a tapping noise just below the window. He pulled the blankets tightly up to his chin and tried not to scream, though he knew that at any moment the window would come down and he would see a hand slide in under the blind. The tapping stopped, there was another deep laugh and he could picture fingers fumbling for the window catch. Then the carriage creaked, the wheels started to turn, they were on their way again and he was safe.

Billy pushed down the blankets and grinned with relief. As long as the train was moving it was all right and there was nothing to be frightened of. Perhaps he'd been safe all the time really and it was just his imagination. After all Mummy and Daddy were in the next compartment and they wouldn't let anybody come in. Daddy was a major in the army. He'd reached 'field rank', as it was called, though that sounded silly, because he worked in an office and had nothing to do with any field. Daddy would stop anybody opening the window.

The train was going quite fast now, the carriage lurching and the wheels clicking sharply on the rails and reminding him of a Burl Ives song. 'Beneath this stone I'm forced to lie, the victim of a blue tail fly.' Billy nodded in time to the clicking wheels and he felt happy because he was going home. He'd liked Berlin at the beginning, but they'd been there far too long. One and a half years, almost a lifetime. Just a few more miles and he could forget about the grey people for ever.

But there might be another stop before the train crossed into West Germany. The seventh stop: the one that mattered, because there was something about seven. The seven days of the week, the seven deadly sins, the seven wonders of the world. He'd better make quite sure that the window was properly fastened just in case they stopped again before the border; the seventh stop.

Billy lowered himself over the side of the bunk, stepping very cautiously so as not to wake Robin, and ran his hand over the locking lever. Everything was all right, it was firmly in position and the blind was tightly drawn down. The train really was going fast too. The jerky tune had changed to a merry hum and the glasses were trembling in their holders above the wash-basin. Billy looked at the door. It would be fun to go out into the corridor for a moment, to show that he wasn't frightened, to prove that there was no danger as long as the train was moving. Besides, Hans might be outside and he liked talking to him. Hans was just a sleeping-car attendant now, but during the war he'd been a Luftwaffe pilot and had shot down over twenty Russian planes. Mummy had told him to take Hans's stories with a pinch of salt, but he enjoyed hearing them.

Putting on his watch, and again taking care not to wake Robin, Billy opened the door and stepped out of the compartment. With the lights winking on the glass panels, and the shiny metal floor, and the blue sign reading 'Toiletten' at the far end, the corridor made him think of a space-ship, a rocket speeding through emptiness. There was no sign of Hans, though; probably he'd gone to have a chat with the guard or one of the other attendants. That was a pity, but if he went to the lavatory and took his time, Hans might be back when he came out. Hans had been on the train when they went to Hanover in September and he'd never finished telling him the story about flying supplies through to Stalingrad. He'd like to hear the end of it.

Very slowly Billy walked down the corridor. Though the heating was on the floor felt icy cold under his bare feet and he gripped the hand-rail to steady himself against the lurch of the train. He stopped outside the lavatory and glanced at the blind covering the window of the outside door. It ran down from a roller and was held in position by a steel catch. Just one turn of that catch and the blind would shoot up and he would know what was really outside. Imagination, or the cold desert with its grey people who stood and waited for the trains to stop.

But no, he couldn't do it. The things behind the window were hideous, unspeakable, that was why the blinds were kept down. That was what the notice was for. Besides, he would be in trouble if anybody saw him. Hans might catch him or somebody might come out of one of the compartments. He looked cautiously at the door beside the lavatory. Number 18. That was occupied by Major Wood. Old 'Timber' Wood, as Daddy called him. He didn't like Major Wood, who had a fierce gingery moustache, always seemed to smell of whisky and pipe-smoke and kept twisting Billy's ear and saying, 'And how's the young hopeful, eh?' whenever they met. If the blind came up with a bang he could imagine old 'Timber' stomping out of the compartment in rank ill temper.

That was impossible, though. The train was making far too much noise for anyone to hear the blind go up, and in the buffet car he'd heard 'Timber' telling Daddy that he was assuring himself a good night's rest with a flask of Haig. 'A bedside bottle for the boy,' he'd called it. 'Timber' would be snoring soundly away and nothing would wake him till Hans knocked them up just before Hanover.

Yes, he had to know what was behind that window. Whatever the risk he had to look out. Very cautiously and with a mixture of dread and daring running through his head, Billy released the catch. The blind slid up quite soundlessly, but the glass was coated with rime and dirt on the outside and he could see nothing except a faint glimmer of light that might have been the moon.

He had to see out, though. He'd risked so much already and he must know the truth at last: whether it was just imagination, or if there really was a desert outside – an icy desert with here and there clumps of squat, prickly trees like the cactus plants Miss Murphy kept in the nature classroom, and always the people who stood and watched the trains. Almost as though somebody had taken hold of his hand he reached out for the locking lever and slid down the window. A blast of cold air beat on his face and made him close his eyes for a moment, but when he opened them he almost cried out with relief.

For there was no desert. There was just ordinary country, the same as he knew at home. The window only came half way down, but through it he could just make out the tops of pine trees and a ridge of hills stretching away in the moonlight. No, there was no desert, but the people might still be there. He had to know if they were just part of his imagination too and there was one way to find out. Quite a safe way, because the door opened against the direction of the train and wouldn't blow back. He turned the handle, pushed open the door, and leaned out into the nightmare.

Two

'Darling, you must try to relax. You must try to take it easy.' Tom Fenwick struggled to put a little confidence into his voice, though he felt none at all. 'They are bound to find Billy soon and he'll be all right. I can't tell you why, but somehow I just know that he will be all right.'

'You say that he'll be all right.' Mary Fenwick didn't look up at her husband. She just stood staring out of the window and her face was dead white under the make-up and had no expression at all. Tom's hand was on her shoulder, and through the costume he could feel her muscles tensed as though under shock treatment. 'Billy has been missing for four hours. We don't know what has become of him, but he probably fell from a moving train. And all you can do is to stand there and say that you know he's all right.'

'Mrs Fenwick, I'm sure that what the major says is correct.' Lieutenant Sutherland was not quite twenty years old and he felt horribly distressed and embarrassed. 'Please let me take you over to the hotel, Mrs Fenwick. Everything possible is being done to find your boy.' He glanced at his watch and then at Fenwick. 'Colonel Baxter has been waiting for over ten minutes, sir.'

'Yes, of course.' Tom followed his wife's set stare. In the thin winter sunlight the tall white buildings of Hanover looked safe and secure and cheerful: fairy-tale palaces mocking his terror. 'Mary,' he said. 'Please go to the hotel with Mr Sutherland. They'll let you know as soon as there's any news. Please do that for me, darling.' He watched her turn and move slowly away, her feet stumbling slightly on the carpet, and then he crossed to the door at the end of the reception room.

'Ah, there you are, Major.' Colonel Baxter of British Military Intelligence made the poor pretence of a smile as Tom came into the office. Under a brown leathery face which was tanned more by spirits than sun and wind, and the brusque manner of the military man who stood no nonsense from anyone, he concealed a very frightened soul. He was feeling frightened at the moment all right. He owed his position largely to the efforts of an ambitious and well-connected wife and he knew that one false move could hurl him into limbo. This business put him in one hell of a spot. If the boy had really fallen from the train he (Baxter) could expect a protest from the East German authorities at any moment, and only last month he had received a memo from London stating that the best possible relations must be maintained before the coming U.N. conference. If, on the other hand, his personal suspicions of what had happened were true, then . . . no, he wouldn't even consider that for the time being.

But this poor devil really was in a state. He studied Tom's face as he came towards him. 'Haunted' was the only word to describe his expression, and it made him think of a song from the First World War. 'I've seen them, hanging on the old barbed wire.'

'Do come in and sit down.' He motioned to the man who stood by the window. 'You know Herr von Zuler, I think.'

'Yes, we are old acquaintances, aren't we, Major?' Kurt von Zuler, liaison officer between the NATO forces and the Spionage-Abwehrdienst of West Germany dragged his steel foot across the floor and he looked what he was: hard and cold and efficient. He smelt slightly of scent, and the hand that took Tom's was bright with rings. 'And may I first say how sorry I am, Major. How very, very sorry about your son.'

'Thank you.' Tom sat down in front of the desk. The wall behind it was almost covered with photographs of Baxter: Baxter in uniform, Baxter in a bowler hat shaking hands with the Queen Mother, Baxter in tweeds with a shotgun under his arm, Baxter sitting in the front row of a cricket team. At any other time he might have found the man's vanity slightly amusing, but not now. Now he felt that he would never find anything amusing again. 'There's been no more news, I suppose?'

'No, nothing of any significance, I'm afraid, though we're getting our noses to what little scent there is. But do you mind if I recap a little for Herr von Zuler's benefit? His department have promised us the fullest possible co-operation.'

'Of course not.' Tom nodded but he didn't understand at all. Von Zuler worked for the counter-intelligence organization. What possible interest could he have in Billy's disappearance?

'Good. Now, let's see where we are.' Baxter studied the map which was spread out across his desk. 'The train left Charlottenburg station in West Berlin at ten forty-five last night. Shortly after it pulled out you and your family went along to the buffet car and stayed there for about half an hour. Correct?"

'Yes, it must have been about half an hour.' Tom tried to throw his mind back. 'Timber' Wood had been going to the rugger match at Hamburg and they'd had a couple of drinks to wish him luck. Mary and he had drunk gin and tonic and the boys Coca-Cola. 'I seem to remember looking at the clock over the bar and seeing it was about eleven twenty when we left to go back to our compartments.' Yes, that was right. They'd enjoyed those quick drinks very much and the kids had had a sleep during the afternoon and were bright and happy because they were going home. Billy had been tensed up about the journey, of course, but there was nothing new in that. It happened every time. Perhaps the poor little devil had had a kind of premonition that something was going to happen to him. Perhaps he'd known all the time. There'd been that odd, stiff-upper-lip look in his face when they kissed him good night, as though he wanted to say something but was holding it back in front of Robin. If only they'd made him tell them. If only Billy had slept with him and Mary with Robin. If only . . .

'And that's about all we really do know for sure, Herr von Zuler.' Baxter's voice cut into his thoughts. 'Major Fenwick and his family get back to their compartments at approximately eleven twenty. Allow about quarter of an hour to say good night and turn in. Correct, Major?' He watched Tom's nod and made a note on a sheet of paper beside the map.

'Yes, after about eleven thirty-five we know nothing. Nothing at all till the train was well across the border into West Germany. Correct again?'

'Quite correct.' Tom lowered his face from Baxter's stare. It had been well beyond the border when they'd heard the tapping. At first he had thought it was the attendant knocking them up, but he'd looked at his watch and seen it was only five fifteen and there was still an hour to go before Hanover. The train was lurching slightly and he'd felt it was just the door rattling till he saw Mary get out of her bunk to open it. As Robin came into the compartment another train had roared past them and he couldn't hear what he was saying. Then it was quiet again and his words had come rushing out. 'Billy's gone, Mummy. Billy's gone – gone – gone.'

'So your son must have left the train some time between about twelve thirty and five fifteen when your younger boy woke up and found him missing.' Baxter scribbled another note on his pad. 'I say twelve thirty because the buffet car closed at midnight and we should allow at least half an hour for the other passengers to settle down after that. Yes, somebody would have been bound to spot him if he'd come wandering out into the corridor before then. If our other theory is true, they wouldn't have risked trying anything till much later than that.'

'Your other theory, sir?' Tom looked up with a jerk. 'I don't understand. Who wouldn't have risked trying anything?'

'We'll come to that in a moment, Major Fenwick, but please help us to clear up a couple of points first. Will you allow me, Colonel?' Von Zuler leaned forward and pencilled two light crosses on the map.

'We've checked with the railway authorities, and during the times in question the train would have been between the western outskirts of Magdeburg in East Germany and Fallersleben, which is twelve kilometres on our side of the border. While passing through East Germany it made no less than seven signal stops. As you probably know, they often halt those trains deliberately to make things awkward for us, but in this case there might have been another reason.' He got up again, staring out at the Hanover skyline with the sunlight glinting on his ringed hand and his face set in a frown.

'Now, Major,' he said. 'Let's dispose of the obvious solution first. You said that Billy seemed anxious before he went to bed? Did he ever suffer from attacks of sleep-walking?'

'No, not to my knowledge.' Tom shook his head. 'When he was very young he used to have bad night terrors, but they seemed to pass by the time he was six.'

'I see. We can rule that out, then.' Von Zuler frowned at the tall buildings as though somehow they might tell him what he wanted to know. 'Yes, a nine-year-old boy,' he said and it almost sounded as though he were talking to himself. 'An imaginative, rather nervous, but perfectly normal nine-year-old boy who vanishes from a train that is passing through East German territory by reason of an agreement made with Russia just after the war. An agreement which is bitterly resented by the East German government, as you well know. It is quite definite that he did not leave the train on our side of the frontier. We've searched every metre of it.'

'But what about on the East German side? Have they searched between Magdeburg and the border yet?'

'They've promised to do so, but we haven't heard anything yet. They've got a fair distance to cover and I don't suppose they'll over-exert themselves on our behalf. Remember that they've been trying to have those trains stopped for years.'

'Excuse me one moment.' Baxter's pencil rapped sharply on the desk. 'Major Fenwick, this may seem a pointless question to you at the moment, but was your son friendly with the sleeping-car attendant, Hans Loser?'

'He knew him. Billy had often travelled on that train and sometimes in Loser's carriage.' Tom stared blankly across the desk. His son was lost. He had vanished from a train without a trace. He was probably dead by now or lying horribly maimed beside some railway embankment. But, though Baxter and von Zuler seemed outwardly sympathetic, he had the feeling that to them his death might not be the worst possibility.

'Billy was a very sociable little boy,' he said. 'He chatted to Loser, that was all.'

'Thank you, Major. They were on friendly terms, in fact. Friendly enough for Billy to have come out of the compartment if Loser had knocked him up during the night and perhaps offered to show him something interesting?'

'I suppose so, but I don't see what you're driving at, sir. Loser could have had nothing to do with it. Why, he was genuinely upset when we found the boy was missing.'

'I am sure he seemed upset, Major Fenwick.' Von Zuler came back from the window, lighting a cigarette as he did so. 'Herr Loser is a glib liar, though not a very tenacious one, it appears.' He put on a pair of thick glasses and pulled out a notebook.

'After the police searched the train, Loser made a statement. He said that between three a.m. and three fifteen he had gone to the kitchen car to make himself a cup of coffee, but apart from that he had not left his seat in the corridor the whole night. He also stated that the blinds on all doors and windows were drawn down according to regulations.

'Well, that story wouldn't hold any water at all.' Von Zuler looked slightly embarrassed as he used the colloquial English phrase. 'If Billy had left the train by the compartment window, his brother is bound to have heard him. At some time during the journey he must have gone out into the corridor and, unless it was between three and a quarter past, Loser was lying.'

'But why? What possible reason could he have had?' In the back of his mind Tom seemed to hear the roar of the train, to see the compartment door open, and Billy come blinking out into the corridor. He could also feel his own nails digging into his wrist.

'Loser says that he merely lied to protect his job. Our police know how to question witnesses and he was persuaded to change his statement after a time.' The German permitted himself a brief smile. 'He now says that as the end compartment of the next coach was unoccupied, he went and lay down in it from one a.m. to five o'clock. When he came back he found one of the door blinds was up. He closed it, thinking he had failed to secure the catch earlier on, and thought no more about it till your son was found to be missing. He at first supposed that the whole story was some kind of practical joke on the part of the two boys and stuck to his version of having been in the corridor all the time apart from fifteen minutes. When it was clear that Billy really had disappeared he was too frightened to alter it.'

'So Billy did fall out through a door. He woke up in the night and walked along the corridor.' Tom could see it quite clearly now.

Billy opening the door to look out, forcing it back against the wind
and peering through the gap. Then he had slipped, or the train had
braked suddenly and he had pitched head first into the night with
the door slamming tight behind him. He could almost hear him
screaming.

'He either fell, in which case the East German police will soon
notify us that they have found him, or something else may have
happened.' Baxter's voice was suddenly very gentle. 'Major Fenwick, by now you must have prepared yourself to hear that your
son is dead. Naturally I hope that that is untrue, but if he is alive,
there may be something which is almost as unpleasant. I want you
to be prepared for that too. Excuse me, though.' He broke off and
lifted the ringing telephone at his side.

'Oh, they are on the line at last, corporal. No, don't put the call
through here. I'll take it next door. Be with you in a moment, gentlemen.' He got up and walked stiffly out of the room.

'And would you like me to finish what the colonel was about to
tell you, Major Fenwick? As it happens it was I who put the idea
into his mind.' Von Zuler's eyes were like blue pebbles behind the
thick glasses and his cigarette was stuck to his lower lip and bobbed
up and down as he spoke.

'I have a suspicious mind, I'm afraid, and when I heard that
Loser had lied about his being in the corridor, I began to wonder if
he had been lying for a rather more sinister reason than he stated.
Our inquiries about him are very incomplete at the moment, but
some of the things we have heard are interesting. It appears that
Hans Loser has recently been in financial difficulties, and also that
he has a mother and a sister living in East Berlin. You see what I'm
implying, Major?'

'I think I do.' Tom nodded, but he didn't really see at all. 'You
mean that Loser may have been working for some East German
organization – that he has something to do with Billy's disappearance?'

'I think he may have done, but as I said, I have a suspicious mind
and we can't be sure till we hear what the Vopo have had to say to
Colonel Baxter. If my theory is correct, however, I think that what
may have happened is this: Loser asked your son to come out of

the compartment during one of those signal stops. He then opened the door of the corridor and handed him over to someone who was waiting outside. Kidnapped him, in fact, Herr Major.'

'Then Billy could still be alive.' Hope surged through Tom's head, but at the same instant he frowned at the absurdity of the idea. 'Kidnapped! But what possible reason could there be? Apart from my pay and a heavily mortgaged house in London we haven't a penny piece in the world.'

'No, you haven't much money, but you must not underestimate yourself, Major Fenwick.' Von Zuler grinned and dragged lightly on the cigarette. 'You have something which may be more valuable to them than money. I have looked through your army record and I understand that your memory for technical data is quite remarkable.'

'Yes, I have a good memory, but . . .'

'No, not just a good memory. A wonderful memory. Almost – how do you say – a photographic memory.' The German nodded approvingly; the headmaster complimenting a favoured pupil. 'And added to that, until last week you worked in the signals office in West Berlin which contains one of the new Haley-Moncelli decoding machines, on loan to your army from the British Foreign Office. We know that certain people in Russia would very much like to know the details of those machines and I am wondering – just wondering – if your remarkable memory could provide them with a circuit.'

'Yes, I suppose I could.' Even as he spoke a diagram swam before Tom's eyes. 'I think I can remember the details of the circuit, but I still don't think they would have gone to such lengths. I mean what about the publicity this will cause? Whatever one hears, these people aren't monsters. And Billy was just a little boy – only nine – nobody would – ' He heard his voice break into a stammer like a cracked gramophone record.

'Yes, only nine, Major. Nine years and three months almost to the day. Poor little boy, but a very important little boy if his father values his safety.' Von Zuler opened a cupboard beside the window and pulled out a bottle and two glasses. 'Ah, I thought Colonel Baxter probably kept something interesting here. We shouldn't really anticipate his hospitality, but in the circumstances . . .' He shrugged his shoulders and limped heavily across to the desk with the glasses in his hands.

'Well, cheers, Major. And let's drink to my theory being wrong – completely wrong. Let's pray that your Billy is just a naughty child who slipped out of a train when it was travelling very slowly and will soon be returned safe and sound to you.' He lifted his glass and knocked back the brandy in a single practised movement as the door opened.

'Sorry. Very sorry to have kept you waiting, gentlemen.' Baxter's normally tight, tanned face looked mottled and puffy and he spoke in jerks as though he had recently been running. He didn't appear to notice that they had helped themselves to his drinks, but flung himself down in his chair and stared at Tom.

'Well, Fenwick,' he said at last. 'I presume that von Zuler has told you his theory and I'm very, very sorry to say that it appears to be correct. The bastards! God, the bloody bastards!' A little tic was beating in his forehead and he raised his hand as though to control it.

'That was East German police headquarters on the telephone. They say that they have searched every foot of the line between Magdeburg and the frontier and there was no trace of your son. The man I talked to, a Colonel Behr, implied that the whole story was a lie; a Western trick to bring discredit on his government.' Baxter paused and blew his nose violently.

'Yes, Major, there are only two possible alternatives, I'm afraid. Either your son has been kidnapped or he has completely vanished.'

Three

'Yes, by all means give me a refill, waiter. Make it a double this time, please.' John Forest, chief correspondent of the Consolidated Press in Western Germany, beamed through the smoke of the cosy little bar. 'And you are sure I can't persuade you to have another, my boy? Quite sure?'

'No, I think I'd better not, thank you, sir.' Lieutenant Sutherland

drew back before his companion's smile. When he had come off
duty a couple of hours ago he'd merely intended to have one drink,
and by the most conservative reckoning he must have at least five
beers and three glasses of schnapps inside him by now. Not that he
hadn't needed them, of course, for it had been one hell of a day.
He'd been called to the office hours before time, and the chief had
been in a foul mood over this business of the Fenwick child. Naturally he, as the most junior commissioned member of the staff, had
been delegated to look after the mother, and he still shuddered at
the memory as he drained the remaining drop of lager in his glass.
'I've had a pretty tiring day, you see, and I don't want it to go to my
head.'

'Yes, it must have been very difficult for you.' As though sensing
his thoughts Forest nodded sympathetically. 'Poor woman. Poor,
poor woman. I can quite imagine the state she must have been in;
broke down in the car and was quite hysterical when you got her to
the hotel. Sandhurst must have taught you a lot of useful things but
not how to deal with situations of that kind, I imagine.'

'No, sir, I never thought I'd have to handle anything like that.'
Sutherland shook his head. Forest really was a decent old boy, he
thought. Friendly and sympathetic and understanding; very different from his chief. When he'd told the colonel how Mary Fenwick
had screamed and sobbed in the hotel foyer till somebody found a
doctor to give her a sedative, Baxter had merely nodded, told him
to go and get on with his work and be sure to see he closed the door
properly behind him. Yes, Forest was quite a different character,
and Sutherland had been delighted and flattered when he'd come
over and joined him in the Europa Bar. An important man, too; one
of the chief Fleet Street correspondents in Germany. There was the
typescript of a long, introspective novel in Sutherland's desk and a
word from John Forest might go a good way to getting it published.

'You know, sir,' he said, 'I think that I will have just one more
beer, if you don't mind.'

'But of course you will, my boy. And also another glass of
schnapps to go with it. Lager beer should be drunk on its own only
in very hot weather.' Forest crooked his finger at the waiter and
beamed on Sutherland like a wicked uncle. And behind the smile

he envied him. He envied Sutherland his youth, and his slim body, and his information. He himself was almost seventy years old, a hell of an age for a foreign correspondent, a hell of an age for any job, if it came to that, and he weighed eighteen stone – most of it sagging puffy flesh which shamed him bitterly each time he took a bath.

But, though he couldn't have Sutherland's body or his nine-teen years, he'd have his information all right. He always got the information he wanted; partly because of his bland, friendly man-ner, and mainly just because he was there. That was the secret of success, the thing that really mattered, the reason the firm would never retire him till he asked them to: just being in the right place at the right moment. He remembered some of the times it had happened: in Berlin when he had seen the smoke from the Reich-stag drifting across the city; off the North American coast when he had been on a ship called the *Morro Castle*; at Pearl Harbour when he had looked up from a breakfast table and heard the first wave of Japanese bombers come roaring in. Just being there when he was needed.

'But I understand that they haven't found the Fenwick child yet,' he said, studying Sutherland's face and noting with approval the slightly blurred expression that alcohol was giving it. He knew that the boy was under oath not to mention anything he heard in Bax-ter's office, and he made his voice sound slightly bored and indiffer-ent. After all, there was no need to hurry: he still had three hours to make the morning editions. Just another drink, just a little more flattery and reassurance and the lieutenant would talk all right.

'No, they haven't found him yet, and between you and me, I don't think they will find him, sir.' Even as he spoke Sutherland knew that he was breaking regulations, but Forest's remark sounded completely innocent and the schnapps made a gentle murmur in his head.

'Really, how very interesting.' Forest knocked back the rest of his beer-chaser. One thing about his swollen body was that it seemed to give him an almost indestructible head for alcohol. Yes, he was on to something good all right. He'd sensed it that morn-ing when his contact at Hanover had telephoned and told him that the military train from Berlin was an hour late. Not that that meant anything, of course. The East Germans were always halting those trains or sending them through on a roundabout route. But when it finally arrived at the station having been searched by the police because a child had disappeared, and the parents had been taken to Intelligence Headquarters, he'd hurried over from Bonn at once. Still not much to go on at that stage, but during the afternoon he learned that Kurt von Zuler had called on Baxter and that the father of the missing boy had worked at the Berlin signals office. Yes, he was on to something interesting, and it was a bit of luck finding Baxter's little office boy in the Europa Bar. He intended to make the most of it.

'But why should you say that they won't find him? Surely if he had fallen from the train in East Germany, the Vopo will recover the body at any moment.'

'They won't, but I can't tell you why I know.' Sutherland shook his head. 'It's all top secret at the moment, you see. All very, very hush hush.' He usually showed great respect for his elders and the omission of 'sir' proved his consumption of schnapps as much as his slurred speech.

'But naturally, my boy, very right and proper of you to keep your own counsel.' Forest nodded approvingly and beckoned to the waiter again. 'Give my friend a refill, please, Herr Ober.

'Now, about that novel you've just finished, Mr. Sutherland. As it happens I'm rather pally with old Bill Seton of the Wayland Press. He's always on the look-out for young talent: why don't you send it to him? – mentioning my name, of course.

'Ah, there you are, Herr Ober. Yes, I will have just a spot more myself as well. Cheers, my boy. Here's to Seton liking – what was the title again? Yes, of course, "Best out of Five"; quite a catchy one.' He beamed across the table, a great jolly Friar Tuck without a sinister thought in his head.

'But what were you going to say about the Fenwick child? Why won't they find him and what do you think really happened?'

'But I told you. I can't say anything. Why, the colonel would have my guts for garters if I breathed a word.' Sutherland stared at his glass. It appeared to be almost empty again though he could only remember taking one sip since the waiter had topped it up.

'Don't be silly, my boy.' Forest's fin-like hand squeezed his arm reassuringly. 'The story is bound to be made public soon, and you needn't worry about Charlie Baxter. I went to school with his father and have known him for years. In any case, you have my word that he'll never know you've even spoken to me.'

'Well, if you're sure it's all right – that the colonel won't find out.' The murmur in Sutherland's head was a dull roar now and he felt slightly sick. 'If you promise.'

'Of course I promise, Mr Sutherland; anything you say to me is as safe as a confession. Now, just you tell me the full story about that missing child and I'll plan a nice letter to the Wayland Press.' Forest propped his huge head in his hand and nodded. 'That's it, my boy, start right at the beginning.'

It took Sutherland over half an hour to tell what he knew and Forest noted every slurred sentence. When at last he had finished he made an obvious excuse and moved heavily away to the lavatory. The light in the cubicle was over-bright and hurt his eyes, and even through the trousers his enormous weight made the seat feel like an instrument of torture. He pulled out a notebook and struggled to concentrate.

But was it remotely possible, he thought? Would even the M.V.D. have done anything like that? Could Sutherland's story be true, or had he got all his facts mixed up and alcohol given them pith?

And even if it were true, would they dare to print it at this stage? He stared at the notebook and shrugged his shoulders. That was the editor's responsibility, not his. His job was merely to tell the story and put it in the most lurid terms he could think of. Yes, a kidnapped child. A child whose father had been in charge of the signals office in West Berlin. That was the kind of angle they needed. A little, helpless child snatched from the train. He hunted for a catch-phrase to start the column. From the Bible perhaps. 'Better that a millstone . . .' No, far too long and flamboyant. Something short was what was wanted here. Something to make people sit up with a jerk as they opened the paper. Yes, that might do very nicely. He pulled out his pencil and began. 'A war on children . . .'

* * *

'Where are they holding him now? How much did they pay you? At which stop was the boy taken from the train? What is the name of the person who paid you, Loser?' The German intelligence sergeant had been shouting the questions for over three hours and he felt almost at the end of his tether. A child, he thought. God, a poor little child and this swine sold him. 'Come on, Loser. Just who paid you?'

'Nobody paid me anything. I had nothing to do with the boy's disappearance. You've got to believe me, Sergeant. For the love of God try to believe me.' Hans Loser swayed against the strap which held him to the chair and without it he would have crumpled to the floor. He wanted the light to stop hurting his eyes, he wanted a drink of water, he wanted a smoke, he wanted the questions to stop, but above all he wanted the bird-like thing in his chest to be still for just a moment. Yes, it was just like a bird. A trapped and terrified bird fluttering madly beside his heart, its wings beating against the cage of his ribs in its efforts to be free and now and again digging its beak into his flesh. He couldn't really blame the bird for wanting to be free, but if only it would stop for just a moment.

'I did lie at the beginning, Sergeant. I was frightened, you see, and I didn't tell them about going into the compartment. I didn't want to risk losing my job. Surely you can understand that. I have a sick wife and . . .'

'Yes, you have a sick wife. You need money, so you sell a child to pay your debts.' Sergeant Schmidt felt anger rising like a pressure gauge. If only I was on the other side, he thought. If only I worked for a force which had no sentimental conventions about human rights, there would be no difficulty in getting this swine to talk. One slow, accurate injection of – what was it – sodium pentothal would bring the truth out of him. Or better still – Schmidt had three children of his own and almost against his will his biceps flexed and knotted. 'Come on, Loser, tell me the truth. Who was it who first suggested the kidnapping to you?'

'There was nobody, nobody at all. How many times do I have to tell you that?' Loser's words were almost automatic as the sergeant stepped round from the desk and walked towards him, his huge body screening the light from his eyes. All he could really think about was lying down on a soft bed and waiting for the thing in his chest to find peace.

'How many times do I have to say that I know nothing? God, how many times?' With hardly any interest he watched the sergeant raise his arm and saw the hand swing down like a flail towards him.

'Stop it.' Von Zuler stood in the doorway and his face was crinkled with disgust. 'You were told to make this man talk, but not by those methods.'

'I'm sorry, sir.' Schmidt turned and looked at him. His voice was slightly slurred and his eyes looked glazed in the harsh lighting. 'I don't know what came over me, but I've been with him for over three hours, and before that Braun and Lang tried. I suppose I lost my temper, but you said we must get him to talk – that he was the one lead we'd got. Questions didn't seem any good, and when I thought about that poor kid . . .' He broke off and stared sheepishly at his hand.

'But perhaps you didn't ask your questions in the right way, Schmidt. In any case nobody ordered you to beat him up.' Von Zuler walked slowly towards the man in the chair. Loser's body was slumped far forward, hanging against the strap.

'Hullo, Hans,' he said and his voice was very gentle. 'My name is Kurt von Zuler and I have come to help you. As long as I remain in this room nobody will raise a finger against you, but you must help me in return. Now, just tell me who organized the kidnapping of the little English boy.' He stared down at Loser and then tilted his face into the light. For perhaps five seconds he studied it and then he turned and looked up at Schmidt.

'Well, Sergeant,' he said, 'you were quite right about one thing. This man was the one lead we had; the one person who might have told us what really happened on that train. It was essential that he should be made to tell us what he knew.' He drew back his hand, the rings sparkling in the light.

'But Loser won't tell us anything at all now, Sergeant. He won't say a word, and would you like to know why? Would you really like to know why?' His voice rose to a shout and his hand slashed out across the man's face. 'Loser won't talk, because you've just killed him.'

Four

Gregor Petrov, Chief of Department Nine of M.V.D., that section of the Soviet Intelligence Organization which dealt with Russia's satellite countries in Europe, was looking forward to his breakfast. For three years after the war he had been attached to the London embassy, and English food had become an essential part of his life. He beamed approvingly at the huge plate of bacon, eggs, mushrooms, two sausages and three – no, better still, four kidneys that his wife laid in front of him.

Yes, he'd been a clever chap when he married Shura, he thought. Not the most beautiful or intelligent of women perhaps, but a very good cook indeed. Though his position entitled him to a couple of servants she would never have allowed another person to prepare his breakfast. The bacon was just the crisp brown texture which he loved and the sausages were pink and bursting, as though inviting the knife. He patted his wife's backside with deep affection as she moved to her own place at the table, and tucked a napkin into his collar in anticipation of the feast.

The first day of November. He noted the date on the copy of *Pravda* neatly folded beside his coffee cup and glanced through the window. Another lovely morning and the Kremlin really looked beautiful at this time of year with the domes shimmering against the clear sky and the walls silvered by frost. Yes, he was very lucky. Just two more months to retirement; he was counting the hours to that day. Already a small villa in the Crimea had been reserved for him and soon he would spend his time lying on a beach or occasionally addressing some minor political meeting and presenting prizes to schoolchildren. The Minister had even hinted that there might be an official recognition of his services too. Not an Order of Lenin, of course. He could hardly expect anything of that sort, but some collective farm or small factory might be called after him. Shura would like that very much, but the important things were still the long idle years of retirement with little to do except potter in the sun and contemplate secure old age and a long, devoted career.

Yes, the future really was bright. Petrov lifted his fork and prepared for pleasure. What should he start with first? A sliver of bacon? A piece of sausage? No, a kidney. His knife slid through the dark, leathery-looking crust to show pale blood inside. Shura knew how to cook them just as he wanted. He raised his fork to his mouth, savouring the faint, scented odour of urine and almost closed his eyes in anticipation. The kidney was within an inch of its destination when the door burst noisily open.

'My dear Tania, how many times must I tell you never to open my door without knocking?' Petrov scowled at his secretary and waved the speared kidney in admonition, but he didn't really feel annoyed. Tania Valina was too appealing to produce anger. At the moment her face was set in a frown of extreme self-importance and urgency, and she seemed slightly out of breath. Unlike Petrov, who regarded himself as a mere civil servant, she revelled in the cloak-and-dagger atmosphere of her job. Her face was thin and very young and with her well-developed body Petrov sometimes felt she was like two people sharing the same house: a pale Madonna upstairs and plump Mother Russia filling the ground floor and basement.

'And what is the idea of bursting in at this time of the morning?' Still brandishing the kidney he consulted his watch. 'Why, it's barely eight fifteen and I'm not due at the office before nine. Like good Party members we should stick to the terms of our agreement.'

'Yes, of course, Mr Petrov, but I thought you should see this.' The girl held out a sheet of shiny grey paper. 'It's a photostat of the front page of the *London Morning Echo*. The Embassy just wired it through to us.'

'Oh very well, if I must, I must.' Petrov popped the kidney into his mouth and reached out. For a moment he glanced idly at the photostat and then his eyes bulged, his face went bright scarlet and he choked. He very nearly choked to death with the scarlet turning to dark purple and his breath gasping out like a steam engine under full pressure. When he finally managed to free himself of the kidney and swig back a cup of coffee, there were tears in his eyes and his forehead was damp with sweat.

'Gregor, I really must insist that you do not work during meals.' Shura frowned at him across the table. 'Your digestion is bad enough as it is. And, as for you, Comrade Valina, you should be ashamed of yourself. You know perfectly well that my husband – '

'Please, please, my dear. Let me think for a moment.' Petrov put on his glasses and studied the paper. 'The bastards,' he said. 'Oh, the stupid, blundering bastards!' He pushed back his chair and stood up, looking sadly down at his plate as he did so. 'Excuse me, Shura. I'm afraid I won't have any time for breakfast this morning.' He turned and walked quickly out of the room with Tania behind him.

'Brr, it's freezing in here. Why can't they get the central heating fixed!' He bent down and switched on the electric fire of his study, seeing himself in the reflector and wincing slightly. Petrov's mother had once said that he had nice eyes and Shura told him he had an attractive smile, but he knew that his face looked as though it had been roughly modelled out of plasticine by a very untalented child.

'Now, get through to Berlin, at once, my dear. Yes, Vopo headquarters, and I want to speak to Colonel Behr. If he's not at the office have them put you through to his private number.' He sat down behind a desk which was almost covered by telephones and stared at the photostat again. The editor of the *Echo* had really gone to town on Forest's story. The headlines 'War on Children' were almost two inches deep and the sub-heading read 'British Child Snatched From Train.' Beside the columns was an extremely savage cartoon of a Russian soldier carrying off a screaming baby.

'Yes, the fools, the stupid brainless fools.' The bronchitis from which he suffered badly gave his voice a harsh, sneering quality that he didn't intend, for if ever a man could be described as having a bark worse than his bite he was Gregor Petrov. 'What sort of publicity will this get us? What can the Minister say at the conference with this hanging over him? And all for an electronic decoder

which will soon be obsolete anyway.' He shook his head in bewilderment as a telephone rang in front of him.

'Gregor Petrov speaking. Yes, of course I'll hold on.' He glanced
through the window as he waited. A few minutes ago it had been
a lovely morning, but now the sky looked grey and heavy with the
promise of more snow.

'Ah, Minister. Yes, I have just seen the English paper and – ' He
broke off before the voice on the line. The Minister was almost
screaming and his words were punctuated by dull thuds as though
he were beating on his desk.

'No, Minister,' he said, when at last there was a break in the ti-
rade. 'As I told you, I have seen a copy of the newspaper and, even
if the story is true, no M.V.D. department had anything to do with
the kidnapping.

'Yes, I quite realize that we cannot afford that kind of publicity
before the U.N. conference, but I can only repeat that we had nothing to do with it.

'No, Minister, I'm not trying to deny that the policy of the
German police is my responsibility, but I really can't be blamed for
an act of pure insubordination. I have a line booked through to
Berlin now and the matter will be given top priority. What's that
you say?' As he listened the picture of a small white villa shone
before Petrov's eyes and faded. Two months to go, but it could be
two thousand years.

'Very well,' he said. 'At least I am grateful that you are so frank,
Minister. Unless the child is returned in good health within the next
twenty-four hours, I will take the full blame.' He put down the instrument and leaned back in his chair breathing deeply. He desper-
ately wanted to close his eyes for a moment and try to imagine that
the whole business was a bad dream, but already Tania was holding
out another telephone. 'Berlin,' she said. 'Colonel Behr.'

'Thank you, my dear.' The instrument felt like a lead weight in
his hand. 'That you, Gustav? Now, tell me quickly. That child which
was taken from the British train: has he been injured in any way?

'What's that?' He grunted as though somebody had just punched
him in the stomach. 'You're sure? Neither you nor your department
had anything to do with it? You're quite sure about that, Gustav?

Could some hot-heads have kidnapped him without central authority, do you suppose? You've checked on that too, have you? But what
about the train attendant, Loser? They say that he was on your pay
roll.' Petrov stared at the photostat as he listened.

Behr claimed that his department had never heard of Loser and
that the railway line had been thoroughly searched and no trace of
the child's body found. In his opinion the whole story was a propaganda stunt; a lie put out by the English. He started to give their
possible reasons for this, but Petrov cut him short.

'Now listen to me, Gustav. In this case I do not believe that the
English are lying and I am quite sure that the child is somewhere
in East Germany; probably alive if the railway line was searched,
as you say. I also think that he may have been kidnapped or, at any
rate, that somebody is hiding him; a nine-year-old boy wandering
about the countryside in pyjamas would hardly go unreported for
long. But, wherever he is, I want that boy found, Gustav, and I'm
holding you responsible for finding him. Yes, we've been friends
for a long time, but if this Billy Fenwick doesn't turn up in the very
near future I shall personally break you.' He replaced the telephone
and looked across at Tania.

'That will set them to work,' he said, 'but I suppose we should
go and look into things ourselves. Yes, book a couple of seats on
the afternoon plane to Berlin.' He stood up and lit a cigarette, feeling slightly better for his threat to Behr, though he knew it was
quite meaningless. If Billy Fenwick wasn't found quickly, it was he
who would be broken.

'But just who is holding the boy, and where is he?' He muttered aloud to himself as he paced backwards and forwards across
the room. The M.V.D. had nothing to do with it and neither had
the East German police or intelligence organizations. He was also
pretty certain that the English would not have made up the story
for any propaganda purpose.

So what had happened and where was he? Petrov paused by the
window. Heavy snow clouds were drifting in from the east and,
though the room was warm, he had a premonition of bitter cold
spreading across the world. 'Where,' he said, pulling his jacket a
little more tightly around him, 'where, where, where?'

Five

The important thing was not to look at the telephone or even to think about it. What she had to do was to try and keep calm, to imagine that Billy was staying with friends, as they'd told Robin, to pretend that everything was all right and smile as though nothing had happened.

Mary Fenwick watched Robin playing on the sitting-room carpet and she fought against the nightmare. He had emptied his toy chest and the contents were spread out in a jumble in front of him; toy soldiers, farmyard animals, a German doll with flaming red hair that he called 'Coppertop', a wooden train. Usually she only allowed him to take a few things out at a time, but now she had to let him do anything he liked. Anything to stop him asking questions, to stop him wondering when Billy was coming home, to stop him thinking about Billy.

It was such a nice room, too: the only room in the house that she'd managed to furnish properly so far. The house itself was a needless luxury, of course. The mortgage payments were far more than they could really afford and there was no reason for them to have a permanent home when they could be moved to the ends of the earth if the army said so. Still, they'd always wanted a place of their own and, when they heard that Tom would be based in London for at least two years, it had been heaven to have a home to come back to. Now she hated every inch of it.

And what almost made things worse was the way everybody had been so kind when they were told to leave Germany. Colonel Baxter had kept patting her arm and telling her to be 'a brave little lady,' and von Zuler had been clearly embarrassed as he broke the news.

'Mrs Fenwick,' he had said. 'I know that you will want to stay in Hanover to be as near as possible to the place where your son disappeared, but, believe me, it is better that you go back to England.' He had put a cigarette into his mouth as he spoke, not lighting it, but fiddling with the matches as though to avoid looking at her.

'If your son really has been kidnapped, and that seems probable now, the people responsible will contact your husband very soon. Because of certain international complications, it is not desirable that they do so in Germany, and I have been asked to put you on the next plane for London.'

Yes, everybody had been kind. The Lufthansa officials had treated them like royalty, and at London Airport there had been no customs formalities and a police car had driven them to Richmond. Now she was back in her own home, safe and secure, with thin winter sunlight glinting through the windows, a fire burning in the grate and her younger son playing happily in front of her.

'The train's crashed, Mummy.' Robin looked up. 'It was going too fast and came off the rails.' He had pushed it against a table leg and the locomotive and carriages lay in a piled heap.

'Yes, poor train.' Mary fought back the lump in her throat and tried to make her voice sound normal and cheerful. 'Put the train away for a rest, Robin, and play with the soldiers now.' Her eyes flickered towards the telephone and then moved quickly away as though the very sight of it might blind her. 'Let it ring,' she prayed. 'Oh, please God, let it ring soon.'

'The telephone will ring, Mrs Fenwick, and when it does, you will both have to be very brave indeed.' The man had been waiting at the house when they got there. An old, stout man with a heavy, aristocratic face, a grey moustache and a thick overcoat which he kept buttoned up though the room was warm.

'I am General Charles Kirk,' he had told them, 'and I represent the Foreign Office Intelligence Service. This isn't really our affair, of course, but as the decoder is F.O. property on loan to the army the Minister felt I should keep an eye on things.' As Mary watched Kirk's mild expression she had felt a sudden glow of hope. On the surface he looked ineffectual, almost foolish, but something told her that he was the man at the top, the man who would find Billy if it were humanly possible.

'Now, let's just run through the facts again, shall we? Looking at the brighter side first.' Kirk had lowered himself into a chair and

Mary had noticed that his left hand was a mass of scar tissue and lacked three fingers.

'The East German authorities have told us that the railway line has been thoroughly searched and no trace of your son was found. That makes it pretty certain that he is alive, and highly likely that somebody is hiding him.

'But do you mind if I smoke, my dear?' He had bowed gratefully at Mary's nod and pulled out a very large cigar.

'Now, the only motive for kidnapping Billy would be to force your husband to hand over the details of that decoder. If the kidnappers are the M.V.D. or the East German Secret Police, I think you have every chance of recovering him in the near future. My opinion is that somebody was told to get the circuit at all costs and took his orders too literally. If that's so, we may not have much to worry about. With a U.N. meeting due to open next month, the Soviet government won't want any adverse publicity, and certain pressures are being brought to bear upon them already. The Americans, for instance, have promised to hold up their wheat shipments to Russia till Billy is returned to you, and very soon all U.K. ports will be closed to their ships. Yes, I imagine that by now Boris Birileff, their Foreign Minister, will have had a few quiet words with the M.V.D. chiefs and somebody will be wishing he had never been born.'

'But you said, if the kidnappers are the M.V.D. or the East German police, sir.' Tom leaned forward. 'Surely they must be. I mean, after all, who else could want to get hold of Billy?'

'Plenty of people, I'm afraid, Major.' Kirk broke off, lighting his cigar and staring up at the grey smoke drifting to the ceiling. 'International spy rings working for money rather than idealism exist behind the Iron Curtain as well as in the West, and it is quite possible that one of these has your son. That decoder is a very valuable piece of equipment, as you know, Major, and your remarkable memory makes you an obvious target for blackmail. And now I want to ask you a question. Think very carefully before you answer it.' His eyes were very thoughtful as he studied Tom's face and his torn hand drummed against the arm of the chair.

'If the persons who are holding Billy were to ring you up at this moment and ask for the details of the decoder, would you give them to them?'

'I'm afraid I don't have to think about the answer, sir.' There was a dark flush on Tom's face. 'In return for Billy's life I would tell them everything I knew.'

'Yes, I was hoping that you would say that, Major.' Kirk smiled approvingly. 'Any normal parent would do so of course, but very few would be so frank with me. As long as you are frank we have a chance, I think.' Once again he drew on his cigar and stared up at the smoke.

'So, you are not only prepared to betray your country, but would kill your child as well, eh?' He waved aside Tom's protest and nodded. 'Yes, you would kill him all right, my boy. Once these people got the circuit of the decoder they wouldn't take any chance of Billy talking. He would be dead and buried the moment they checked that your information was correct.'

'Then what can we do? For God's sake, General, is there nothing we can do?' Mary could feel tears running down her face but she hadn't got the strength to lift her hand and wipe them away.

'No, my dear, I'm afraid there is very little that we can do. There is, however, a great deal that the Russians can do; if they can be persuaded to help us.' Kirk pulled out a rolled newspaper from his pocket.

'As I said before, a great deal of pressure has already been put upon the Soviet government: the stopping of the American wheat supplies and the embargo on their ships entering our ports. There are also certain unofficial pressures which they won't like at all. Have you seen the midday edition yet?' He held out the newspaper showing headlines that read 'Paris Riots – Soviet Embassy Stoned'. The editor's comments on the Russian denial of the kidnapping were mild and reasonable, but slashed across the foot of the page in scarlet letters were the words 'Prove It.'

'No, Comrade Birileff won't want to go before the United Nations with that kind of thing hanging over his head and, if we can keep the pressure up a little longer, I think that every Soviet agent and East German policeman will be looking for your son.' Again Kirk reached in his pocket and produced a long envelope.

'We have to give them time, though. Time to decide to help us, which will go very much against the grain, and time to get to work. You will have to supply that time, Major.'

He tore open the envelope and drew out a sheet of foolscap covered with figures and symbols.

'Now, unless my experience is worthless, I am sure that the people who are holding Billy will contact you before another day is past and demand the details of the decoder in return for his life. This is what you will give them.' He held out the paper. 'It is a slightly altered version of the first stage of the circuit, but without the other three stages nobody could know it is valueless. Before handing over the other stages, you will demand proof that Billy is well; a letter in his handwriting and a photograph. That will get us a little of the time we need.'

'But that's all, General? That's all we can do?'

'Yes, I'm afraid that that's all that can be done at the moment.' Kirk smiled at Mary as he stood up. 'I can't promise anything, but I think it will work. As you know, your telephone has been disconnected for all except foreign calls, and you will just have to wait for it to ring.' He tightened his coat and moved to the door. 'Goodbye for the present and try not to worry. I am quite sure that it will ring very soon.'

'Mummy, Mummy, when is Billy coming home?' Robin's voice broke into Mary's thoughts and she looked up with a jerk. 'He's been away so long now, Mummy.'

'Yes, darling, it has been a long time, but he'll be coming back soon.' Again she struggled to hold back emotion, but this time it was no good. She just couldn't keep it up any longer.

'Oh, darling, come here,' she said. 'Come to me, my little boy.' She pulled Robin to her, feeling his hair against her cheek and hearing nothing except her own sobs. For almost a minute she held him like that and then very gently pushed him away from her and stared across the room. Already Tom had got up from the sofa where he had been lying silent and motionless and was walking towards the little table by the window. On it, harsh and strident and threatening, like the opening bars of some very macabre modern symphony, the telephone had begun to ring.

* * *

At the top of a tall office building in Berlin, Major 'Timber' Wood paced the floor of his room like a huge caged animal. It was Sunday afternoon and, apart from a janitor in the basement, he was quite alone in the building and from time to time cursed angrily to himself to relieve his feelings, which were a mixture of compassion, self-pity and sheer murderous rage. At the moment rage was very much in the forefront.

'You bastards,' he said to the filing cabinets at the side of his desk. 'You bloody, unprintable bastards.' He turned and aimed a kick at the waste-paper basket and stumped back to his chair.

'A kid,' he thought bitterly. 'A poor, innocent, little kid.' They'd pay for it all right. If the government had one ounce of guts between them, the blasted Russians would be paying for it now. 'Timber' was too young to have taken part in the Korean War and had never heard a shot fired in anger in his life. A number of highly trained experts had attempted to show him the probable nature of any future world conflict, but their efforts had fallen on very stony ground. He still thought in terms of past glories; pennon-bearing tanks lumbering across the desert and massed infantry waiting to charge. 'Over the top, Sergeant. Give them a taste of the bayonet, lads.' 'Timber's' present command consisted of a pay corps corporal and three German clerks, but at the slightest nod from High Command he would have cheerfully hurled them at the Berlin wall.

Compassion. Yes, he felt a lot of that. Tom and Mary Fenwick were old friends and he'd been fond of Billy too. A funny little blighter, a bit shy and withdrawn at times, but with a most appealing smile. Strange – no, terrible to think that it was just the other day that he'd squeezed his ear and wished him good night on that damned train.

And where the hell was he now, and who had him? No, 'Timber' didn't even want to think about that, remembering lurid boyhood reading of blackmailers posting their victim's ears with the demands for ransom. Once again a picture of massed British infantry charging the Russian hordes flickered through his mind.

But self-pity was there too, for he had been on the train bound for the greatest honour of his life. The New Zealand rugby team had been touring Germany and he had been selected to play for a Combined Services fifteen against them. The moment the kidnapping story broke, all Berlin personnel had been ordered back to their posts and here he was behind his desk with the match played and lost without him.

Not that there was any reason for him to be at the office, of course. Sunday afternoons usually found him in the Marlborough Club, but he didn't fancy the place any more. It was full of reporters who kept asking him for his views on the kidnapping or how well he had known the Fenwicks. He'd almost taken a swipe at one of them last night.

No, work was the only thing that could help him take his mind off Billy, and he bent over the files on the desk. Colonel Mackenzie's account was overdrawn to the tune of a hundred and ninety-two pounds three and eightpence at the close of yesterday's business and Lieutenant Smith's three pounds and a penny. He'd have to be very tactful with the colonel, but one-pip lieutenants were quite a different matter. It would do Smith a power of good to be told exactly where he got off. He slipped a sheet of paper into the typewriter and then frowned as once again he heard the noise in the outer office.

Damn Herr Schlott! He'd promised to have the catch of that door fixed days ago and there it was, rattling as though in a full gale. Probably Schlott had forgotten it on purpose to annoy him. The man had been sullen, almost rude at times since he'd torn a strip off him for being late last month. He'd have something to say to Herr Schlott in the morning.

Rattle, rattle, rattle. No, he couldn't stand much more of that. 'Timber' pushed back his chair and stumped out to the reception office. With the lights off and the sky outside dark with snow clouds, the covered typewriters and filing cabinets looked slightly sinister and threatening objects in the gloom. The door was fastened, though. He had to give Schlott his due for that, but it was rattling all right – banging rather, as though somebody or something was beating against it. That was quite impossible, of course.

Walther, the watchman, was the only other person in the building, and he'd have rung the bell if he wanted to speak to him.

Someone was there, though, or something. He could hear the sound of quick breathing through the woodwork and the rattle was more like a scratch at times, as though an animal were trying to get in.

'Timber' had few nerves in his big body, but he felt a slight twinge of trepidation as he slid back the catch and pulled open the door. It turned at once to pain and astonishment as a small figure who appeared to be dressed in rags hurled itself into his arms, treading hard on his toes as it did so.

'You,' was all he could say for a moment, staring down at the tear-stained face that was looking up at him through the dim light. 'My God, it really is you.'

'Yes, yes, it's me. And please, please take me home, Uncle "Timber",' said Billy Fenwick.

Six

'Darling, Billy's home, that's the only important thing. We've got our son back.' Tom Fenwick leaned forward and kissed his wife. 'He's safe and well and nothing else matters.'

'Yes, I suppose so. I suppose he is well, but why doesn't he tell us exactly what happened and where he's been?' Mary glanced over Tom's shoulder towards the door. Billy had been asleep for hours. He'd dropped off almost as soon as she tucked him into bed. She'd looked in at him at least six times and Tom was right: there was nothing to worry about, nothing to be frightened of any more, and she had to control herself and stop tiptoeing upstairs and peering in at him. All the same . . . 'We're his parents, darling,' she said. 'It's our right to know what happened to him.'

'And Kirk has told us that it's far better that we don't know – that Billy tells us nothing.' Tom leaned back on the sofa and lit a cigarette. The events of the day were still like a vague dream to him. The phone ringing, the operator announcing a call from Berlin, his hand reaching for the false circuit Kirk had given him and to his astonishment 'Timber' Wood's voice on the end of the line saying, 'Hold on, old boy. I've got somebody who wants to speak to you.' Then the room had seemed to tilt and there had been a great roaring in his head as he had heard Billy's voice. 'Daddy, Daddy, I'm with Uncle "Timber". Please come and take me home, Daddy.'

After that everything had happened very quickly and there had been more calls. From the duty officer at Tempelhof promising that transport for Billy would be laid on as soon as possible, from Colonel Baxter, finally from B.E.A. in London saying that the plane was on its way.

Kirk himself had taken them to the airport, uniformed police holding back the crowds who had gathered in the little suburban road and the newspaper cameramen who were trying to break through the cordon and get a shot at them. Though Kirk's car was provided with a motorcycle escort it had been driven slowly and sedately along Western Avenue, and his cigar and an enormous heater had made the atmosphere barely supportable.

'Well, my dear,' he had said to Mary, 'that's it. All's well that ends well, eh? Your Billy is coming home, but there's no credit due to ourselves or the Russkis. There was no kidnapping either. He fell among friends, you see, and it's rather a touching little story.

'As far as we can make out – the boy's account is very incomplete and I'll explain why in a moment – this is what happened.' As he spoke Kirk had stared sadly out at the drab wilderness of the western suburbs: mean houses and small factories, and a thin layer of snow already turning to slush.

'It seems that Billy was unable to sleep on the train and at half past two – he is very definite about the time – he got out of bed and went into the corridor. There he opened a door.

'Yes, my dear, I know it was a very strange and disobedient thing to do, but he said that he had to see outside. He told our chaps in Berlin that he thought there were some kind of ghostly people standing beside the railway line and he had to prove he wasn't afraid of them. Quite a normal childish fantasy in the circumstances, I imagine.

'At any rate, he opened that door and leaned out. As he did so, the train braked violently and threw him forward on to the step.

He managed to hang on there for some time – he has no idea how long, but finally his grip gave way and he dropped off.'

'And he wasn't injured, General? You are quite sure he wasn't injured?'

'No, apart from a slight concussion, he wasn't hurt at all and he is a very lucky boy indeed. The train must have been travelling slowly when he finally fell from it and he landed in a snow-drift, though he caught his head on something and was knocked out for a while. When he came round there was a woman bending over him.

'Billy was terrified at first, of course, but the woman was obviously friendly and, when he told her what had happened, she talked to him in English and took him to a house where he was given food and put to bed.' Kirk knocked an inch of ash from his cigar.

'And that's all that Billy can, or more probably will, tell us. From the time he reached that house, to when he found himself outside a West Berlin underground station near Major Wood's office, he says that he can remember nothing.'

'You say, "more probably will tell us," sir. Why should he lie or hide anything?' Tom glanced through the window. They were almost at the airport now, with signal gantries glowing against the evening sky.

'I've no idea, my boy, and our Berlin people won't venture an opinion as to whether he is lying or really has lost part of his memory.' Kirk pulled out a gleaming half-hunter watch. 'In a few minutes you can ask him yourselves, but I don't advise it. Children hate breaking promises, and I think your son made a very solemn promise indeed.' He replaced his watch and leaned back against the cushions.

'Both of you have lived in Berlin and you must realize what things are like in East Germany since they put up the wall. Before then, there was at least a sporting chance of getting out, if you were prepared to give up all your roots and possessions, of course. Now, there is no hope at all, except for the few; the very, very few, Mrs Fenwick.' Kirk had smiled at Mary, but through the smile Tom had seen how tired he was; too much worry, too much responsibility, too many decisions to be made.

'Yes, a very few people manage to get out nowadays, my dear. The handful who know and run the escape routes to the West: tunnels under the Spree River, basements extended into the Allied sectors, ways through the sewers and the disused railway tunnels where the barriers have been removed.'

'And you think that Billy was taken into West Berlin by one of those routes?'

'I can't be completely sure, Major, but in my own mind I'm almost certain that he was.' The lights glinted on Kirk's face as the car purred through the tunnel to the Central Airport. 'To me there seems no other possibility and this is what I imagine must have happened.

'As I said, Billy is a very lucky little boy. He fell into a snow-drift and he also fell among friends – powerful friends; people who run, or at least know about, one of those escape routes. When they discovered who Billy was, they helped him in every way and finally smuggled him into West Berlin. In return for their help, he promised to say nothing about them or what he had seen. Please don't make him break that promise, my dear. Believe me, the fewer people who know about those routes, the better it is.'

'I won't make him break it, General. All I'd like to do is to thank them for helping him.' Mary's words sounded almost automatic as though she were barely listening. Slowly and unhurriedly, as though speed were somehow too vulgar for its vast gleaming bulk, Kirk's car slid towards the main arrival building . . .

Midnight. The little clock on the mantelpiece started to strike and brought Tom back to the present. 'But, darling, you haven't been questioning Billy, have you?' he said. 'You haven't been pumping him – not after your promise to Kirk?'

'Yes, I've been pumping him, as you call it, Tom.' Mary frowned. 'After all, I am Billy's mother and I have a right to know what happened to him. And I'll tell you this, Tom: that child is terrified of something. I sensed it as soon as I saw him at the airport. Somebody has frightened him badly.'

'You think so? I must say it wasn't the impression I got. To me he almost seemed to be cocky.' Tom tried to recall exactly how it had been. The big gleaming hall with the reporters held back by a rope barrier and a group of officials hurrying to greet Kirk; the P.R.O. of the airline, a police inspector and somebody with the unlikely name of Sir Mason Toyne; a sense of waiting and expectancy, and then a door had opened and Billy had come into the hall.

And cocky really was the word to describe his manner. Billy had stood in the doorway for a moment, holding the hand of an air hostess, and then had run towards them. As he had run he had looked at the reporters, and the group beside Kirk and Tom had seen a fleeting look of pure pleasure and self-importance on his face, as though to say, 'Here I am, gentlemen, back from the dead. This is what you've been waiting for; the big moment.'

'Cocky!' Mary turned on him like a blight. 'Don't you realize that his manner was just an act, a pretence to try and show that he wasn't frightened? Tom, I'm his mother and I intend to find out exactly what happened to that child and why he is terrified out of his wits.'

'Yes, my dear, you've remarked several times that you're his mother. You are also a suspicious, over-imaginative woman and a demon where your children's welfare is concerned. There is nothing wrong with the boy; nothing at all.'

'Do you believe that, Tom? Do you really believe it? You may have been right about Billy's manner at the airport, but didn't you see his shoulders when he had a bath? They were covered with flea-bites.'

'And so what?' Tom suddenly felt as tired as Kirk had looked in the car. 'Isn't "flea-bite" a popular expression for something completely trivial and unimportant? I don't doubt for one moment that Billy has been in some pretty unsavoury places, but I still think that we owe nothing but deep gratitude to the people who helped him.'

'Do we? I wonder.' Mary got up and paced across the room. 'Darling, I may be crazy, but I'm sure something horrible happened to Billy. When I had put him to bed I asked him to tell me who were the people who had looked after him and he sort of cringed away as though I were about to hit him. I told him not to be silly and he looked up and said, "Mummy, please don't make me tell you. Please don't ask me. If I say anything, Hans will know and come for me. Iron Hans knows everything."'

'Hans?' Tom frowned. 'Did he mean Loser, the sleeping-car attendant? His name was Hans.'

'No, it wasn't Loser. I asked Billy that and he said, "Don't be silly, Mummy. Not that Hans. I mean Iron Hans. Little Iron Hans who can destroy the world." His voice sounded like a frightened old man's.'

'Got it!' Tom's frown changed to a grin. 'Iron Hans is a fairy-tale character, of course; from Grimm, I think, and Billy was reading it last term. You remember: the wild man covered with brown hair whom they find in a pool and shut up in an iron cage. Billy reads a lot and has far too much imagination, like his mother. He was just having a game with you, darling.'

'Perhaps you're right. I hope so, at any rate. And now let's go to bed. I've had about all I can take these last few days.' Mary gripped his arm as they walked upstairs, stepping very softly so as not to waken the children, but on the landing she paused and pushed open Billy's door. As she did so, Tom saw her body go rigid, and the next moment he was beside her with his hand reaching for the light switch.

Billy was sleeping heavily, with his head sunk deep in the pillow, and he appeared natural except for two things. His right hand was tearing and kneading at the sheet, and he was snoring. It wasn't like a child's snore. The noise he made didn't even sound human: it was a deep, grunting, coughing noise with a rasp and a whine in it which might have been made by some worn-out piece of machinery dragging an enormous burden up a steep hill.

'The thermometer, Tom. Get me the thermometer. It's in the dressing-table drawer; the top one on the right.' Mary's hand was on the child's forehead, but he didn't wake up. He just lay there quite naturally, apart from his clutching hand and the terrible guttural rasps of his snore.

'Have you got it?' She unbuttoned the pyjama jacket and slid the thermometer under Billy's arm, pressing it tight against the instrument while her other hand reached for his pulse. She didn't need a watch to tell her how fast it was, while all the time his snore rattled around the room, filling it.

'That should do it, darling.' She pulled out the thermometer, holding it to the light and shaking her head in disbelief as she did so. Her face looked much the same as when she had gone into the sleeping compartment and found Billy missing three days ago.

'Tom,' she said at last. 'Tom, this can't be true. Look for yourself.' She swayed against the bedpost as she handed the thermometer to him. 'As far as I can see, his temperature is over a hundred and seven.'

Seven

'The flowers that bloom in the spring, tra-la . . .' Sir Marcus Levin, K.C.B., F.R.S., sang loudly and tunefully as he swung his Ferrari on to the dual carriageway and opened her up. 'Breathe promise of merry sunshine.'

Seventy miles an hour, eighty, ninety, a ton up, as the motorcycle maniacs called a hundred. Sir Marcus grinned fondly at the dashboard dials, revelling in speed and the sound of his rich baritone voice. 'As we merrily dance and we sing, tra-la . . .'

A hundred and ten now, and it felt as though he was barely moving. Very nice indeed, he gloated. Probably the nicest car that he, or anybody else for that matter, had ever owned. Almost seven thousand pounds' worth of car, but cheap at the price when one considered twelve cylinders, fuel injection and a custom-built body ordered to his own specification. He'd come a long, long way in his forty-five years.

'We welcome the hope that they bring, tra-la . . .' He negotiated a roundabout in an expert racing glide and charged up the next hill with his silencers blasting the early morning mist. 'Of a summer of roses and wine.'

Yes, a hell of a way he had come. All the way from his father's and grandfather's little shop in Lemberg, and most of it had been hell itself: a road to Calvary. He could remember the battle of the Warsaw ghetto, the Ruhr labour camps and Belsen. He could remember how he had slaved all day in a London factory and washed dishes every evening, trying to save a little money and praying that a British medical school would accept him on the strength of his single year at Warsaw University. After that had come the struggle for his degree and the fellowships at Cambridge and Edinburgh and New York, won in competition with men who had ten times his advantages of background, and would have left him standing if it hadn't been for his talent and ambition and Rachel. Yes, Rachel had always been beside him, urging him on.

Then, years later, he had knelt down in a big glittering room and felt a sword touch his shoulder. At that moment, he had seemed to see an old bearded face smiling at him and had had to fight to stop himself from saying aloud, 'Here I am, Father. Here I am, Jakob Levinski. Almost at the top, almost where you said I should go.' That had been the happiest time of his life, but it didn't last long. Three months later Rachel had died in a Vietnamese jungle, because the American plane which was supposed to have brought medical supplies had carried nothing except munitions and anti-Communist posters.

'Of a summer of roses and wine.' No, he didn't want to think about Rachel now. He'd loved her, he'd married her, and he'd dug her grave in rotting vegetation, because a little commonplace bug which penicillin could have wiped out in hours had burned her up. Rachel was only a memory and she wouldn't have wanted him to think about her. As she'd often said, only his career and his future mattered to her and, though he'd come a long way, he still had further to go. Sir Marcus Levin, Knight Commander of the Bath, Fellow of the Royal Society, and if he still wasn't recognized as one of the really top bacteriologists in the world, he very soon would be when his paper on the Enterin 165 Virus was read next month. Marcus Levin, who knew that he had been as emotionally and spiritually dead as old Marley's door-nail since the day that Rachel left him. He stopped singing as the car breasted the hill and whispered, 'To hell with the flowers that bloom in the spring.'

Still, it was going to be a nice day. Already the sun was climbing over the Surrey hills, the Thames valley was opening up in front of him, and wreaths of mist were drifting like smoke around the squat tower of Guildford Cathedral. He'd cursed when 'Jacko' Jackson had rung him up at six o'clock in the morning and asked him to come over to Richmond as a personal favour, but he felt quite pleased now. Not that he could ever have refused 'Jacko', of course. The man was his oldest friend, probably the best male friend he had ever had, though their relationship was eccentric to say the least. The bitter, ambitious Jew with a chip like a sack of cement on his shoulder, and the hearty, beer-swilling captain of the hospital rugger fifteen who had never suffered very much in his life and was called 'Jacko' not merely because his name was Jackson, but because his face resembled that of an amiable chimpanzee.

But 'Jacko' was wrong, of course. He had to be wrong, because his diagnosis was beyond the bounds of credibility. What he had seen in that child was merely a complicated case of pneumonia. 'Jacko' had jumped to conclusions and that was why he was a struggling G.P. earning about half the average national salary, and *he* was Sir Marcus Levin with fifty thousands pounds' worth of assets to his name and, like the car, worth every penny of them.

'Mark, old man, I've never asked you for many favours, but I'm begging for one now,' 'Jacko' had said. 'I don't want to call in the County Officer yet, nor even Redford Smith at the hospital, till I'm quite sure what it is. Please come over and give me your opinion, Mark. I hate to admit it, but I really am very worried indeed.

'What's that? Oh, yes, I've tried an injection of Genomycin; half a gramme just over an hour ago. There's been no change that I can see, though. Surely it should have started to lower his temperature by now?'

And 'Jacko' should have known better than that, of course. He couldn't even have been reading his *Lancet* lately. There had been an article on the antibiotic he'd used only a few weeks ago and it would take no effect for at least two hours from the time of administration. By now it should be working, though, and already the fever would be down and the breathing getting easier. When he got there the kid would probably be well over the crisis.

But it was getting pretty late. Marcus glanced at the dashboard clock. He'd promised 'Jacko' he'd be with him by seven and it was five past now. Damn Mrs Anderson! She'd seemed to think that her duties as housekeeper included those of a nannie in charge of a delicate and delinquent child. He'd crept downstairs in his socks, but she must have heard the telephone and was waiting by the dining-room door, tall and gaunt and imperious in a blue tartan dressing-gown.

'No, Sir Marcus,' she'd said, as always using the title with a flourish. 'It may be a matter of life or death, but you're not leaving the house till you've got something warm inside you. No, I'm very, very sorry, but I don't care if your new car has a dozen heaters in it. Now, just you go into the dining-room and wait for me, Sir Marcus.' He'd fretted for ten minutes while she prepared coffee and two boiled eggs and then stood grimly by the sideboard to see that he ate them.

But he was almost there at last. He swung the car into Richmond Park, narrowly missing a stag which was crossing the road, and he suddenly felt very glad that he had come. Apart from the pleasure of doing old 'Jacko' a good turn, apart from the lovely morning, there could be some useful publicity in the case. That Fenwick child had made the headlines once, and there was a good chance that he might do so again. Already he could picture them. 'Pneumonia Strikes Kidnapped Boy. Sir Marcus Levin Consulted.'

And here he was: Number 32 Park Approach with 'Jacko's' battered old Morris parked well out from the kerb. He drew up, picked up his case, and climbed purposefully out: a tall, imposing figure in his black coat, his Homburg hat and the thin sunlight glinting on his pearl tie-pin.

'Doctor . . . ?' Tom Fenwick opened the door almost as he touched the bell and tried to force his face into a smile. 'Dr Levin?'

'Yes, I'm Levin.' Marcus disliked professional soldiers on principle and normally would have put him in his place with 'Sir Marcus Levin', but he saw that this poor devil was on the point of collapse. 'My friend Dr Jackson asked me to come over and have a look at your boy; just to give a second opinion, you understand.' He bowed slightly and stepped into the little suburban hall, taking off his coat as he did so. He had cultivated a manner for every occasion and now radiated confidence. 'Doctor's here, so stop crying. Sir Marcus has arrived and there's no more need to worry. Everything will be all right because the expert has taken charge.'

'Now, Major Fenwick,' he said, studying Tom's face as he handed him his hat and coat. 'I understand that the patient is upstairs and

I'll find my own way. And, while I'm making my examination, I want you to go and get a good, strong, alcoholic drink inside you; brandy, if you have it. Yes, that's an order, Major.' He turned as he heard 'Jacko's' voice at the top of the stairs and ran boyishly up to meet him.

'Mark, thank God you've come, old man.' 'Jacko's' face looked pinched and his handshake was clammy. 'I can't begin to say how grateful I am.'

'That's all right.' Once again strength and confidence gleamed in Marcus's eyes. 'Only sorry I couldn't get here earlier, but my dragon of a housekeeper insisted that I swallowed two large eggs before she let me out of the house. Now, let's have a look at your patient. He's in here, I suppose.' He started to move towards an open door on the landing.

'No, no, he's in the room at the end there. We put the mother in that one. She was hysterical, Mark, and I had to give her a sedative. It took the nurse and the husband to hold her down.'

'Take it easy, Jacko. Surely that was perfectly natural under the circumstances. The poor girl must have been under a hell of a strain lately. First the disappearance of her child and now this – this pneumonia, or whatever it is.' Marcus studied his friend with genuine concern. The old chap really was looking dreadful. He'd be needing a bit of medical attention himself if he didn't try to relax.

'Now, tell me about the kid. You gave him a shot of Genomycin two and a half hours back. The fever is a bit easier, I suppose?'

'No, Mark, it's no easier.' Jackson shook his head. 'Five minutes ago the temperature was still over a hundred and seven.

'Mark, I'm not an expert like you. I'm just a poor bloody G.P., but I'm prepared to swear that whatever is killing that boy is not pneumonia. Apart from the fever and the lung congestion, there are other things.'

'Well, let's have a look, shall we? And take it easy. Whatever happens, it can't be the end of the world.' Marcus frowned slightly. He didn't like the word *killing* at all. Now that he had arrived on the scene, 'Jacko' should feel that his worries were almost over. 'From what you told me of the case, everything points to pneumonia with complications. Exposure after he fell off that train, the time factors, the lung congestion and the vomiting. Still, even the best of us make mistakes and he certainly should be reacting to the antibiotic by now.' He pulled open the door and walked into the room, nodding to the nurse by the bed and sniffing the faint tang of antiseptic, corruption and oxygen.

'Thank you, nurse.' He leaned forward as she removed the little oxygen mask and studied Billy Fenwick's face. No, not at all a bad-looking kid apart from rather buck teeth which needed a brace. He was still snoring, but not very loudly, and there was a greyish tinge in the flushed cheeks. Marcus put his hand on the boy's forehead and sniffed his breath, like a terrier at a rat-hole.

'No,' he said. 'No, I think you may be right in saying that it isn't pneumonia. You've had a specimen of the sputum sent over for analysis? Good, that should tell us what we're up against at any rate. Let's have a look at these spots you mentioned. Probably a heat rash, I should think. He's almost burning up, isn't he?' He opened Billy's pyjama jacket and as he did so he stiffened. No, he thought, it's not possible. You're jumping to conclusions like 'Jacko', because it's your own subject. This child has never been out of Europe – it can't be possible. He pulled out a lens and studied the spots. They were rather beautiful: a ring of dark-red roses sprinkled on the pale skin.

'Tell me,' he said, 'was this rash there when you first examined him?' He looked at Jackson, but it was the nurse who answered.

'No, Sir Marcus.' She obviously enjoyed using the title and her voice had a comforting assurance similar to his own. 'It started to come up about two fifteen. His fever was very high then and I was sure it was just a sweat rash.'

'A sweat rash. Well, let's hope you're right, nurse. My God, I hope you are right.' The time factor was one thing in their favour at any rate. If what he suspected were true, the spots should have been the first symptom, not the second. Once again he stared down through the lens, praying that his suspicions were groundless, but as the tiny red blotches swam into perspective he knew that there was no mistake. The last time he had seen anything like them he had had to travel four hundred miles by jeep and helicopter and on horseback.

'Is there a telephone on this floor, nurse? In the next bedroom. Good, I don't want the father to hear what I have to say. Please go and get through to the County Health Officer. And hurry.' He shook his head at the question in her eyes and pulled down the bed-clothes.

'And now, let's see, Jacko. Let's see if we really have a monster to deal with.' He ran his hand over the child's body, over the flat belly, past the tiny, undeveloped genitals and into the crotch, searching for the thing that he dreaded to find: the hall-mark which belonged to the greatest killer in history. It was there all right, just as he knew it would be, hard and throbbing under his fingers, and he could al-most feel it growing. About as large as a walnut now, soon it would reach the size of a small orange and then burst. When it did so Billy Fenwick would probably be dead.

'Yes, Jacko, we've got our monster, I'm afraid.' Marcus stood up and went to the wash-basin, soaping his hands very carefully. 'No, there's not much point in replacing the oxygen mask. Give him a full adult shot of tetracyclin. I don't suppose it will do any good at this stage, but – ' He shrugged his shoulders and walked out of the room. All jauntiness had left him and he looked much older than his forty-five years.

'Got him for me? Thanks.' He took the telephone from the nurse, lighting a cigarette as he did so. 'That you, Dr Lawrence? Yes, Marcus Levin here. What's that you say?' His voice was sud-denly strident and foreign; the wailing of Israel against all Aryan stupidity.

'Yes, Doctor, I do realize the time, but I have not the slightest in-terest in the fact that you are just out of your bath. You will not ring me back, but listen very carefully to what I have to say.

'This is absolutely top priority and I am speaking from 32 Park Approach, Richmond, in connection with the Fenwick boy whom you must have heard about. I want the house isolated at once and you had better get on to the Foreign Office and the Ministry of Transport. We must round up all the boy's contacts of the last few days. As soon as I've put down this telephone, ring the Chief Con-stable.

'What's that, Dr Lawrence? Oh, yes, I think you can safely call it a national emergency.' He looked up at the nurse and nodded. 'You see, unless I'm wrong, we've got a case of bubonic plague on our hands.'

* * *

Plague – bubonic plague – *bacillus pestis* – the Black Virgin as they had called it — the Dark Lady of the Middle Ages returned to an English suburban street in the second half of the twentieth century to trouble the world. It was impossible, it had to be impossible. 'Jacko' Jackson shook his head in disbelief as he crossed the road towards the Bear Inn. The promise of a fine day had faded soon after nine o'clock, just about the time that Billy Fenwick died, and heavy clouds were drifting in with the promise of rain. Already a few drops were falling on the pavement.

Bubonic plague. He himself had known that it wasn't a case of pneumonia. But bubonic! Could old Mark really be certain at this stage? He revered Marcus Levin more than any other human being, but he didn't see how Mark could be so sure. Even with the rash, the bubo in the groin, and the lung congestion, nobody could be quite certain till full laboratory tests were made.

And where could the child have picked up the bug, if it came to that? Jackson ordered a pint of beer and carried it across to his usual seat by the saloon bar window. If he had been out East – India or China, say – it would have been understandable, but there hadn't been a case of plague in Europe for years; unless you counted that chap from the research establishment near Salisbury not so long ago. Besides, if Mark was right about it being bubonic, it was acting very strangely. The rash and the swellings should have been the first symptoms and the lung congestion should have come later as a side effect. Jackson had not been a brilliant student, but at least he remembered that much.

Still, it wasn't his affair any more. His patient was dead, they'd removed the body, and the public health people had taken over. A decontamination squad had been at work when he left the house, the parents and the other boy had gone to the isolation hospital and the street outside had been almost blocked by police cars. Mark had driven off to the Central Laboratories soon after Billy died, and there was nothing for him to do except go home, attend to his practice and nurse his inoculation shot.

It had taken all right, that was one thing at least. He could feel his arm throbbing painfully as he lifted the tankard. He shouldn't really be drinking on top of it, of course, but a couple of pints wouldn't do any harm and he'd felt like stopping at the Bear before going home. The place was just beside the Laneham Park Rugby Ground and the members used it more as a club than a public house. The landlord was a former Welsh international and there were silver trophies along the top of the bar and the walls were covered with photographs of fifteens. He himself appeared in three of them. Apart from one enormously fat man chatting to the barman, the room was empty and Jackson was glad of that. Though the matter was no official concern of his any longer, he had to think about it.

Plague. The worst killer in history. Knocked out whole populations almost overnight: Marseilles, London, Bombay. Naples, where they had disinfected the sewers and blind rats had come pouring out into the streets. Right back in the Bible, too: the end of the Philistines and the Assyrian army dying before Jerusalem. Manson-Bahr had said that was malignant malaria, not bubonic, but many authorities still disagreed with him.

Tetracyclin would stop it, if you got your patient in the early stages, of course, but they'd have to find every contact of the boy's and also the source of infection. Take a hell of a lot of doing. He glanced up as a board creaked a few yards away from him. The fat man had left the bar and was examining the photographs on the walls, nodding as he recognized a familiar face.

They'd have to be careful about security, too. The very word 'plague' carried the hint of panic and civil disorder. Already the newspapers would have heard that something was happening in Park Approach, and if the story broke before the original carrier was located, things could be pretty ugly. Yes, Lawrence had better have a good tale to fob them off with.

'Excuse me, sir, but am I addressing Dr Jackson?' The fat man had paused by his table and was beaming down at him. A whisky glass looked like a thimble in his great flabby hand.

'Yes, I'm Jackson.' 'Jacko' started to frown with annoyance at the interruption, but the man's expression was so friendly and pleasant that he had to smile back. 'I'm afraid I –'

'No, you don't know me, Doctor, but I know you all right – by reputation, of course. W. L. R. Jackson, the finest centre three-quarter Laneham Park ever had.

'But may I join you for a moment, Doctor? I would also count it an honour if I might buy you a drink.' He crooked a finger at the barman and lowered his vast bulk into a chair.

'Yes, this really is my lucky day, Doctor. Dr W. L. R. Jackson. The great W. L. R. Jackson.' He fumbled in his pocket and produced a visiting card. 'My name is Forest – John Forest – and I once saw you score three tries at Twickenham.'

Eight

'Come in, General Kirk, and welcome to my rather untidy castle.' Marcus Levin smiled and held out a beautifully manicured hand. 'We're all at sixes and sevens at the moment, I'm afraid, but at least pull up a chair and try to make yourself comfortable.'

'Thank you.' Kirk looked suspiciously around the office in the Central Laboratories and then relaxed. Though Levin seemed a flamboyant, over-dramatic fellow and his room was a maze of papers and scientific equipment, it was at least warm. He unwound his muffler and lowered himself into a chair by the desk.

'Now, Sir Marcus,' he said, 'before you try to put me in the picture, I should like to say that I shall quite understand any resentment you may feel about having an ignoramus on scientific matters hanging at your heels. No, it's true enough.' He waved aside Marcus's polite gesture of protest. 'My medical knowledge is confined to what is in *Dr Goodall's Family Physician* and I'll just have to try not to get in your way. The fact is that as the child appears to have picked up this – I don't know if "bug" is the right expression – in East Germany, it was decided that my department should co-operate with the health authorities.'

'I know that, General, and believe me, I appreciate your co-operation very much. We're going to need every bit of help we can get.' Marcus frowned at the papers on his desk. 'I gather that the Germans are rounding up all the boy's contacts and having them immunized.'

'All his contacts from the time he reached West Berlin. Before that we don't know whom he contacted, or rather who contacted him. The Minister has spoken personally to Moscow, however, and they've promised to do all they can to trace the boy's movements from the moment he fell from the train.' Kirk grinned slightly. 'Adversity makes strange bedfellows, as they say, and our friends behind the Iron Curtain don't want an epidemic of plague any more than we do.'

'But why haven't they got one, that's what I want to know?' Marcus's hand beat sharply on the desk. 'That child was bitten by an infected flea and he can't have been the only one. Somewhere, in East Germany probably, though it's not my job to say where, that bug, as you call it, is on the rampage, and unless we can find every carrier and, what is more important, the original source in the very near future, we're in real trouble.

'General Kirk, I wonder if you have any idea of the speed at which this thing travels? I've seen it myself in India and East Africa and it's quite frightening. The original carrier is usually *Xenopsylla cheopis*, of course, but, once established, droplet contact with an infected mammal . . .'

'Just a minute, Sir Marcus.' Kirk broke in shaking his head. 'I'm afraid you are going a bit fast for me. Could you just give me a general and very simple account of the working of this thing, *bacillus pestis*?'

'I'll try, but at this stage, we're not even sure that it is *bacillus pestis*.' Marcus slid a photograph across the desk. It showed a pink surface lightly dotted with what looked like small oval capsules stained purple.

'Now, General. That is a piece of animal tissue infected with the bacillus of true bubonic plague. The propagation and spread of the disease is carried out in a most beautiful manner.' He got up and paced in front of Kirk like a lecturer before a class.

'The bacillus lives in the body of the rat flea, *Xenopsylla cheopis*, which suffers no ill effects from its presence. The flea bites its host, however, the rat is infected, leaves its hole and dies. After a period of about three days, depending on climatic conditions, the flea, which relies on fresh blood for its existence, leaves the carcass of the rat and attaches itself to man and other animals. The incubation period in the human body is a further three days, after which the breath of an infected person can transmit the disease. The average mean duration of illness in fatal bubonic plague is five and a half days, making a total of eleven and a half for the full cycle.

'And now I'd like to show you something else.' Marcus slid another picture in front of Kirk. It looked almost the same as the first, though the capsules were stained a darker purple and they bulged slightly at one end like pears. 'As I said, eleven and a half days is the cycle of true bubonic plague. This little chap appears to take rather less than five.'

'And that's what killed Billy Fenwick? You mean it's not bubonic, as you thought?'

'Yes, that's what killed him, General, and though it's certainly some form of Eastern plague, it's like nothing I've seen or heard about before. Apart from the time sequence, it doesn't act like true bubonic. In normal cases the rash and the bubos, the swellings, should come first and the pulmonary congestion follow them as a side effect. That didn't happen with the Fenwick child. The damned thing is behaving in a way it has no right to do – no right at all.' Marcus scowled down at the photograph as though the creature's unorthodox behaviour were a personal affront.

'And what's it doing in Central Europe anyway? That's possibly the strangest thing of all. The fleas that carry bubonic are parasites of the black rat, which is almost nonexistent except around a few dock areas. The most accepted theory is that it was wiped out by the larger brown variety: *ratus Norvegicus*, as it is wrongly called, which is usually free of them. That's why plague epidemics are so mercifully rare today. An attractive thought, isn't it, General? A war for the life of mankind being fought out in cellars, and sewers, and garbage heaps.'

'Yes, I suppose you could call it attractive.' Kirk was still staring at the photographs. 'But tell me, Doctor – sorry, Sir Marcus. These bulges in the second picture. What are they?'

'I just don't know, General Kirk, and please call me Doctor. I much prefer it.' Levin smiled, but his mind was far away, studying the bacillus through Kirk's eyes. 'I have a theory about them, but it's terribly far-fetched and I'd much rather discuss it when we have more facts to go on.

'Excuse me, though.' The telephone rang shrilly on his desk and he leaned forward to answer it. 'Oh, yes, please put him through at once.' He cupped his hand over the mouthpiece and looked at Kirk. 'It's the Semmelweiss Isolation Hospital in West Berlin. Major Wood, the man who found Billy Fenwick, was taken there this morning. It appears that they didn't manage to get him inoculated in time.

'Ah, good evening, Dr Heller,' he said in German. 'Yes, Marcus Levin here. He died, did he? I see, an hour ago. Yes, I was expecting that, but I didn't think it would be so soon.

'What's that? What's that you say, Doctor?' As Marcus listened, Kirk saw his hand tighten around the instrument.

'And you're sure about that? The tetracyclin had no effect whatsoever? It didn't even slow it down in any way?

'I see. Yes, of course we'll come up with something else in time. We're bound to. What I'm worried about is how much time have we got. Anyway, thank you for ringing, and I'll be in touch as soon as I have more news from our end. Goodbye, Doctor, and all the luck in the world.' He replaced the telephone and stared across the room for a moment. All his urbanity had left him and he suddenly looked what he was: a middle-aged Jew grown old before his time, who had almost been beaten to death in two concentration camps.

'General Kirk,' he said at last. 'I think I should put all my cards on the table. When I first examined that child, I thought that we had a slight variant of Eastern plague to deal with. I thought that the infection had probably taken place before the boy left the train, but the father assured me that there were no flea-marks on his body that night.

'All right. I was still more curious than bewildered. I had a species that developed faster than usual. *Bacillus pestis* often throws up strange variants. I could also accept the lung congestion coming before the rash and the bubo as some strange union of the bubonic and pneumonic forms of plague.

'But this!' He craned forward over the second photograph again, and there was the trace of a foreign accent in his voice which only happened when he was excited. 'These swellings you saw, and the fact that the bacilli are resistant to tetracyclin – the most effective antibiotic we have for the Pasteurella group – that makes me wonder if we are up against something unnatural: some kind of man-made mutant, in fact. Remember that the last person to die of Eastern plague in this country was a scientist working at the Porton Research Establishment.'

'You mean germ warfare, Doctor? If we are working on those lines, isn't it possible that the East Germans are doing so too?' Kirk shook his head and he sounded much more confident as he came to a familiar subject. 'Yes, it's possible, I suppose, but highly unlikely. I'm pretty well informed about what goes on in East Germany and I haven't heard of any such establishment.'

'Then either your information is incomplete or we've got a natural freak to deal with.' Levin broke off frowning as the door opened. 'What is it, Wilson? I told you we weren't to be disturbed for the next half-hour.'

'I know that, sir, but I think you had better look at the last slides we prepared.' Marcus's assistant could scarcely contain his excitement. 'Those bulges seem to be what you suspected. They are definitely opening . . .'

'The devil they are!' Marcus was already moving to the door. 'Yes, you were quite right to interrupt me. You'd better come too, General. We may be going to see a piece of living history.'

'Now, which is the earliest slide?' He glanced impatiently at the row of microscopes on the laboratory desk. 'The second from the right. Good.' He bent over the eye-piece, turning the fine adjustment till the picture slid into focus. As he did so, he could feel beads of sweat breaking out on his forehead.

For though it was thought to be impossible, though it was against the evidence of every recorded case, it was happening and he was watching it. He was looking at a miracle that might make his name live as long as medical textbooks were read.

The things were dead, of course. The stain had killed them and, before they died, some of them had been dividing, reproducing themselves asexually. That was normal enough, but in the right-hand corner of the picture there were others which had not behaved normally at all. They had split open at the bulged ends to release a tiny, almost transparent speck which drifted beside them in the purple dye.

'We now come to sporulation in bacteria, gentlemen.' In the back of his mind Marcus could hear an old, bored voice delivering a lecture he had probably given a hundred times before. 'The process of spore formation found in certain bacteria is a method of self-preservation. When placed in conditions where death would normally result, these organisms develop enormous powers of resistance and can remain dormant but alive almost indefinitely. If the spores are later returned to circumstances where the bacillus can grow, alterations take place in their structure, they germinate and normal reproduction is resumed.

'This process however is confined to certain species only and I am happy to say that *bacillus pestis*, for example, is not one of them. If it were, there is every probability that you and I would not be here today.'

But this culture was sporing. There was no doubt about it. Through the next microscope Marcus could see the whole surface of the slide covered with those tiny drifting dots. He tried to remember all he knew about plague – all he had learned in nineteen years of sweat and study and often incredible danger. None of it helped him at all.

The plague epidemics of classical times. At Alexandria where fifty thousand inhabitants had died almost overnight; at Carthage and Athens and Byzantium – all those outbreaks had been well documented, the symptoms laid out because, though no proper clinical methods existed, there were men of curious and scientific mind to record them. In China and India too there were records and, after the microscope was invented by van Loeuwenhoek, bacteriology had become a science.

Yes, almost all the major outbreaks had been recorded. All except one outbreak: the big one, the longest one, the one that had probably killed fifty million people and changed the economic structure of Europe. The symptoms had seemed to point to plague: tumours, dark patches which opened like mouths, vomiting from the lungs, but nobody could be certain what it was. There had been no accurate accounts because it had arrived in an age when reason was dead and men lived by superstition. Marcus lit a cigarette, dragging hard at it, and then turned to the third microscope. Wilson had added a different stain to the slide and the spores were much more visible – little reddish pinpoints floating around their parent bodies like moons.

No, they hadn't studied anything except dogma in the fourteenth century, and nobody could be completely sure what the epidemic had been. Its coming had been heralded by earthquakes, drought and dense fog. They had called it an act of God at first, and afterwards a sickness of the earth because the rats and mice came pouring out of their holes to die. They had said that cats, the creatures of the Devil, were responsible, and they'd killed them, allowing the rats to multiply. Then at last they thought that they had discovered the true cause: the well poisoners; and the pogroms had begun. Fifty thousand Jews killed in Burgundy alone, rabbis crucified head down like Peter, children hurled into the flames because their parents refused to allow them to be baptized.

But was it possible that the outbreak had not been true plague at all, but this – the thing he was looking at now? The means of self-preservation were there, and could it have lain dormant for centuries and then woken up for him to find? 'Sir Marcus Levin, the discoverer of – the isolator of – ' As he considered the possibilities, the immunization shot in his arm seemed to burn and swell. It appeared to have taken all right, but was he really safe? Could any normal serum stop something which had managed to maintain itself for six hundred years?

'General Kirk,' he said. 'I think I may be on a completely wrong track . . . I hope I am, but I'd like you to look at this.' He drew back and motioned Kirk towards the microscope. 'If my very vague suspicions are correct, we have a real devil to deal with. Can you see them?' He watched Kirk fiddle with the adjustment and nod.

'Good. Now, look at the end of the rods. Can you see how they have split open and released spores? That was thought to be scientifically impossible, but you can see it happening, can't you?

'Well, I don't know what we're up against yet. I've only got a hunch at the moment, but if my hunch is right those things should have died six hundred years ago.' His hand came up and gripped Kirk's arm. 'I think that what you are looking at could be a return of the Black Death from the Middle Ages.'

* * *

It was really raining now. The clouds that had gathered over London in the morning had solidified into a huge, dark tent and there was not a breath of air. The rain dropped straight down out of the sky and bounced off the street and pavements like a forest of steel spikes standing upright.

'Your car should be round in a moment, sir. I sent a message to your chauffeur in the parking lot.' Marcus had said goodbye to Kirk in the laboratory and Wilson, his assistant, was escorting him out.

'Thank you, Dr Wilson.' Kirk's hat and muffler were at last adjusted to his satisfaction and he drew on a pair of thick gloves.

'Oh, I'm sorry. It's Mr Wilson, is it?' Kirk glanced keenly at him. Wilson was still young, barely in his middle twenties by the look of him, but his face was very intelligent. 'Just how long have you worked with Sir Marcus, Mr Wilson?'

'Seven years, General. He took me on as a lab. assistant after I left school.' There was a gleam of hero-worship in his eyes. 'I've been all over the world with Sir Marcus: India; Africa; Vietnam, where his wife died.'

'Yes, I've heard about that.' Kirk scowled out at the rain. It showed no sign of slackening and the gutters reminded him of brown mountain streams.

'Now, about this business of the bacillus producing spores. As I told Sir Marcus, I'm an ignoramus on medical matters and I understood very little of what he said. I did gather, however, that this sporulation, as you call it, has never been met with before in cases of plague.'

'No, General, it has never been met with before and that's what makes the whole business so incredible. It's like a creature suddenly changing its whole pattern. Almost as though you and I should start to grow another finger on our hands.' Wilson blushed scarlet as he remembered the torn talon on Kirk's left wrist. 'Oh, I'm sorry, sir. That was a stupid example.'

'It's quite all right.' Kirk smiled at him. 'I only wish I could grow another three on one of mine. But to get back to this plague mutation or whatever it is. A deadly disease – probably the most deadly disease there is – discovers a method of preserving itself almost indefinitely. A very nasty thought indeed. And what about the Black Death theory? Because there are so few records between the years 1342 and '88, Sir Marcus has put forward the possibility that this thing might be a return of the Black Death bacillus which, through its spores, has managed to maintain itself dormant but alive for more than six centuries. Do you agree with his view, Mr Wilson?'

'Do I agree?' Again Wilson reddened. 'Look, General Kirk, I'm just Sir Marcus's lab. assistant – his bottle-washer, if you like. It's not for me to question his judgment. After all he . . .'

'Yes, I know all that. Marcus Levin is an internationally known bacteriologist, but I'm still asking you, Mr Wilson.' A big pennon-bearing car had pulled up before the entrance, but Kirk ignored it. 'You have been trained in the subject, and I want your personal opinion. Has Sir Marcus any real scientific basis for saying that this may be a return of the Black Death bacillus?'

'I just can't answer that, General. This bug we've got is a freak. There's never been a case of sporulation in *bacillus pestis* before. Until we've had time to study it and also found the source – the first carrier – we can't be certain what it is. We don't know much about the Black Death either, if it comes to that. It was always thought to be a species of Eastern plague, but nobody can say for sure.'

'Thank you, Mr Wilson. That answers my question, I think.' Kirk nodded. 'There is not enough evidence at the moment to be certain about anything and Sir Marcus has jumped to conclusions.'

'Yes, I suppose you might say that, sir.' Wilson looked horribly embarrassed. 'The subject of the Black Death has always fascinated him; became a sort of personal challenge, if you like. He may have given it undue prominence in this case. All the same, he is a very fine scientist and I think we should trust his judgment.'

'You may be right, Mr Wilson, but thank you for what you've said.' Kirk held out his hand and smiled.

'And don't worry about it, my boy. You haven't been disloyal to your chief because you've told me nothing that I didn't suspect myself. Goodbye for the time being.' He turned and hurried down the steps to his waiting car.

'Thank you, Martin. Yes, it's back to the office again, I'm sorry to say.' He nodded to his chauffeur and leaned far back on the seat listening to the thunder of rain upon the roof.

Yes, he thought, Marcus Levin probably was jumping to conclusions. Even the most brilliant minds sometimes bypassed reason and gave way to unscientific hunches. And, if Levin were wrong, it meant that he could be wrong too. The thing might very well be a man-made mutant produced at some germ-warfare establishment which he hadn't heard about. He'd put every agent they had in East Germany to try and trace it, and he'd also have to talk to somebody in Moscow. He hated the very thought of that, but if there was going to be an epidemic there was no doubt that he'd get a hearing. After all, Russians and Germans could die of plague as easily as British children. The probability was that some fool of a scientist had let a culture get loose and was keeping quiet to protect his own skin. If so, the M.V.D. would soon get the truth out of him. The real drawback to the theory was the question why no cases had been reported in East Germany before now.

There was also the problem of the Fenwick child's contacts before he arrived at Major Wood's office. Colonel Baxter was convinced that he had been smuggled into West Berlin through one of the escape routes and the child's garbled version backed him up. It would be difficult to find the people who controlled the route, but it would have to be done. If Baxter didn't come up with a lead soon, he'd have to go to Germany himself.

And for the time being, the whole business had better be kept dark. Nothing had been released to the Press yet and it wouldn't be till they had more facts to go on. Kirk stared out at the evening crowds hurrying through the rain to buses and tube stations. The very word 'plague' had a ring of panic and they mustn't be told anything till the authorities were quite sure what they were up against. Panic! Apart from the riots and pogroms of the Middle Ages, there had been religious mania too: crazy theories that flagellation and sexual activity were its preventives; men and women copulating in the streets while others flogged themselves in graveyards.

No, there would be no public announcement till they knew exactly what they had to deal with. He pulled out a cigar and very carefully sliced off the end. He was just about to light it, when his eyes seemed to blur and he was sitting bolt upright shouting to his driver to stop.

At a newsvendor's stand at the end of Waterloo Bridge were two placards. They were already sodden with rain, but the word PESTILENCE was clearly visible on each of them.

* * *

That night, a man and a woman in Berlin, two men in London, a small child in Hanover and a soldier in Paris were starting to rot. They didn't know what was happening to them and neither did Iron Hans. He just sat in his cage and grinned.

Nine

'I agree, General Kirk. If this information is correct, and I stress the word "if", we must bury our differences for the time being.' The telephone was attached to a loudspeaker and microphone and Gregor Petrov paced up and down before the window as he spoke, staring out at the blizzard that was covering Berlin. As in London, the weather had promised to be fine at first, but at noon it had begun to rain and by early evening the rain had turned to sleet. Now thick snow swirled and eddied around the trees and the lamps of the Unter den Linden and was beginning to settle. Petrov

liked watching the snow. It almost made him feel he was home in
Moscow.

'Yes, General, a thorough investigation is being made at our
end. You have my word for that. I would also like to say how much
I – I – ' he struggled for the correct English word – 'how much I appreciate your speaking to me personally. I quite realize the embar-
rassment it must have caused you. Now, if you will just hold the
line for a couple of minutes.' He switched off the microphone, but
continued to stare out of the window. At least the snow is clean, he
thought. Antiseptic drops of frozen moisture blanketing the earth
and purifying it. That was rubbish, of course, but it made him feel
slightly better to think about it. His own body was stale and damp
with sweat, and the meal he'd eaten two hours ago was sour in his
mouth.

Plague, he thought. Bubonic plague. In a bad epidemic thousands could die almost overnight, he'd heard; die horribly too: the
bodies swelling, turning black and bursting like fruit that had been
left to drop from the tree. Rats were supposed to be the carriers,
weren't they? Scaly bodies wriggling through a hole in the wall,
tearing open sacks of grain, fouling the contents, contaminating
everything they touched. That stuff he'd eaten this evening: Königs-
berger Klops it was called; a typical Berliner dish. He'd enjoyed it
very much, but were the ingredients all right? The meat, the flour
that made the thick creamy coating, the sauce and the vegetables?
Yes, a horrible death. Dark swellings in the flesh splitting open and
starting to stink. Petrov struggled to push the thought out of his
mind and turned back to the desk where Tania Valina was standing beside a tall man wearing the uniform of a Vopo colonel. He'd
worked with Gustav Behr for years, he called him by his first name,
but he didn't feel that he really knew him. Though Behr was always
polite, always friendly, there was a coldness in his manner which re-
pelled intimacy.

'Well, Gustav,' he said. 'You heard what this Kirk implied; is
there any truth in it? Have your government, unknown to us, been
carrying out experiments in bacteriological warfare?'

'They have not.' The German's pale, rather scholarly face was
almost devoid of expression. 'There have never been any such ex-

periments in East Germany and no research establishment exists for the purpose.'

'Thank you.' Petrov nodded. 'So this – this thing, whatever it is, is not a man-made product from our side of the Iron Curtain, as they call it. On the other hand, if it is a natural outbreak, why have no more cases been reported by now? Either Kirk is lying or something very strange is going on.' He looked at Tania and grinned.

'And where do you think it comes from, my dear? From outer space, perhaps? Is it possible that the Martians are an extremely intelligent race of microbes who have just invaded us?' He shuffled back to the telephone, feeling slightly better for his little joke.

★　★　★

Less than three miles away from Behr's office, a woman named Ruth Eulenburg was trying to get to sleep. She wanted to sleep very badly because it was far the best cure for influenza and she was in for an attack all right. She'd felt it during the morning: aching joints, headache, and a throat that felt as though it had been scraped with a file. She'd done everything to stop it, taken huge doses of Vitamin C and aspirin and gone to bed, but the 'flu was winning hands down.

If only Wilhelm were with her it wouldn't be so bad. If only he hadn't gone away. From the bedroom walls the face of her husband seemed to stare across at her. If only Wilhelm would come home soon.

That was crazy, of course – the fever playing tricks with her mind and her eyes. Wilhelm couldn't ever come back. A bullet from a Vopo rifle had torn open his chest and he'd died in her arms. It might have been only yesterday when they'd come through. The old lorry lined with boiler plate and scrap iron lurching down the Muskauerstrasse towards the wall which had not been mortared then, and they'd gone slap through it. Seventeen of them lying in the back and Wilhelm crouched low down over the steering-wheel. For a moment the barbed wire had seemed to hold them, but somehow the lorry had torn over it, with the bullets thudding harmlessly against the iron plate, till they came to rest beside an American sentry box. She'd twisted her ankle as she jumped from the back and ran to the cab, wrenching open the door and shouting at the top of her voice, 'Darling, we made it – you made it – we're free – really free and in the West at last!' Then Wilhelm's body had fallen sideways and she'd seen the blood pouring from a rent in his coat.

Well, Wilhelm was dead. He'd died a hero and there was no point in thinking about him any more. She just had to concentrate on fighting off the 'flu because there was so much work to do. Another group would be coming through the new tunnel to the Ku'damm station next week and she had to make arrangements for meeting them. The Vopo would be bound to find it soon, but they should get a dozen parties through first. It had been a risk bringing that child out by it, but Gretel knew her business and was sure he wouldn't talk. She remembered how he had sobbed in her arms at the junction and she'd had to comfort him for half an hour before he promised to go and find the English major's office.

Yes, she had to be all right in the morning. If only she could sleep through, if only the aspirin would start to work, if only her head would stop throbbing, if only she could breathe. Ruth reached out and switched on her bedside radio. The little green dial glowed comfortingly and a Munich beer song thudded in time to her pulse. 'In der Nacht – schläft der Mensch – nicht gern alleine . . .' It died and an announcer's voice took over. 'Good morning, ladies and gentlemen. The time is now exactly one minute after midnight and before continuing our programme of light music, there is a news flash from London. The British Ministry of Health report that . . .'

'No, no, please God, no.' Ruth heard herself muttering aloud against the voice.

'All persons in any country who think they may have been in contact with this child are urged to get in touch with their doctor immediately.'

'No, no, no.' She was out of bed now, staring at her face under the dressing-table lamp and feeling sweat pour from her body and grow cold.

'I repeat that there is no cause for alarm as long as all contacts are inoculated.'

'No, no, it can't be true. It mustn't be true.' As the announcer broke off and a dance tune took over, Ruth staggered to the telephone. Somehow she seemed unable to control her hands and it took her a long time to dial the number she wanted.

'Professor Klee,' she said when at last somebody answered. 'Herr Professor, I know that I am not supposed to ring you, but I'm sick and I have to talk to you . . . No, no, please listen.'

Klee's voice sounded metallic and he appeared to be talking gibberish; something about a wrong number and replacing the telephone. He was obviously trying to protect himself, but she had to make him understand.

'Herr Professor, haven't you heard the news yet? About the little English boy that Clever Gretel sent us? We have to talk to her, Herr Professor. We have to know her real name, so we can find out exactly where the boy came from. Tell me her name, Professor Klee. Gretel – Clever Gretel . . .'

'This is the exchange. You have dialled a number which is unobtainable. Replace your instrument and re-dial please.' The West Berlin postal authorities were extremely proud of their recorded-instruction system, but Ruth Eulenburg still shook her head in disbelief. 'I know that you're there, Herr Professor, so listen to me. We must contact Gretel at once. We have to know what happened to that child. Gretel, Herr Professor. Clever, Clever Gretel . . .' Her knees buckled and she fell to the floor, dragging the telephone with her.

She was still repeating the name when they found her in the morning and she kept on repeating it in the ambulance. Just before she died she tried to say it again, but by that time she was too weak for anybody to hear her. 'Gretel – Gretel – Clever Gretel.'

Ten

'A ring, a ring of roses, a pocket full of posies . . .' Marcus Levin hummed as he watched the rats. He had sent his assistants off to an early breakfast, wanting to concentrate by himself, and he was quite alone in the laboratory.

'Atishoo, atishoo, we all fall down.' Almost every nursery rhyme recorded an historical event, and 'A Ring of Roses' was true to type. The animals in the first cage had been infected at six o'clock in the evening and they were dying already; one of them lying on its side and kicking feebly while its partner's efforts to escape were slackening at every minute. Marcus glanced at the clock and made a note on his pad. 'Though no accurate information is at present available in human subjects, the duration of the disease appears to be approximately three and a half days. In the case of rats . . .' The kicking had stopped now and the first animal was quite still. 'Twelve and a half hours.' Incredible but true.

A miasma, a contagion sent from the stars to infect the earth, the ancients had considered plague. A sickness of the soil which drove the creatures up into the daylight to die. That was happening in front of him, as he knew it would, though he hadn't expected the extreme violence that went with it. The six cages had been built to resemble underground sets, lined with clay and bricks and having a single exit blocked by three light wooden partitions. In every cage except the first the rats were still struggling to escape, tearing madly at the barriers and at each other in their efforts to get out. The big cross-bred albino in the fifth cage had killed its smaller neighbour and was busily gnawing at the second partition, though its strength seemed to be on the wane. Would human sufferers react with such violence, he wondered? 'Jacko' had kept the Fenwick child quiet with sedatives, but his hand, tearing and kneading at the bedclothes, appeared to imply that. He added another note on his pad. 'For the first seven hours after infection no apparent change in the animal was observed, but this was followed by a three-hour period of intense physical activity, aggression and the urge to escape. After this the organism slowly ran down into coma and death.' Marcus left the cages and bent over a microscope. A hanging droplet system had been used instead of dye and the things were alive and busily at work, dividing and reproducing themselves as was natural, but also preserving their race for posterity which they had no right to do. Even as he watched, more of those tiny dots burst from the parent bodies and circled around them: spores which in certain circumstances could lie dormant for centuries till moisture reached them, the creature awoke and became active again.

And had it happened like that? Was this a return from some past outbreak that had managed to maintain itself over the years, or was his original idea of a man-made mutation right, for all Kirk's assurance that no research establishment existed in East Germany? Marcus was strongly drawn towards the first possibility, though he had no real scientific grounds for this, but merely a hunch, an intuitive feeling. What he had to do was to study the thing and find the most efficient way of controlling and destroying it. The normal inoculation serum for bubonic seemed to be working all right, that was one point in their favour at any rate. The boy's parents and younger brother had been caught in time, though two more cases had been reported in Germany: the air hostess of the Lufthansa plane, and Major Wood's housekeeper. They'd have a job tracing all their contacts before it turned up again.

But even with effective inoculation, could they hold it back? The worst thing about orthodox plague was the speed at which it travelled, eleven and a half days from the beginning of the cycle to death of the patient, and this thing took less than five.

And they had found no antibiotic to touch it yet. He peered into the next microscope. Penicillin had been added to the culture but the creature was still thriving. They'd have to find the original source soon, or whole populations could be wiped out almost overnight.

The publicity wouldn't help either. Since those headlines 'Pestilence' had blazoned the news to London, the radio and television networks had issued sober and reassuring statements, but he doubted if they would be enough. Unless it could be announced that the outbreak was under control, public confidence would be at breaking point before long.

But where could that damned child have picked up the bug? Who was the original carrier? Marcus crossed to a shelf at the back of the room. Half his reference library on plague had been sent over to the laboratories and it was piled high with books. Sticker's *Die Geschichte der Pest*, Creighton's *A History of Epidemics in Britain*, Bulard's *De la Peste Orientale*. He grinned sadly at the titles. Sticker and Creighton and Bulard had been trained observers, men of science who had patiently recorded every detail. What would they

think of his blind intuition? All the same, none of them had seen
anything like the little monster which was working away behind
him. He opened a map of Central Germany and frowned down
at it. Somewhere along that twisting roundabout line between
Magdeburg and the border Billy Fenwick had fallen from the train.
Somewhere in the area he must have met the carrier.

Magdeburg, Oberfeld, Raltona, Rudisheim, Helmstedt. Marcus's finger ran along the route and then stopped. Rudisheim? Just
what did he remember about the name? Where had he heard it before? From the map it appeared to be a small unimportant town or
just a village, but somehow it rang a loud bell in his memory. He
pulled out a heavy leather-bound volume from the pile of books.
Vogel's *The Great Pandemic of the Middle Ages*, translated into English by Nevison and Butt. Translated pretty inaccurately too. He'd
always intended to buy an original edition, but somehow he had
never got down to it. At least the index gave him what he wanted,
though, and he flicked open a page. Yes, here it was.

> The outbreak of plague at Rudisheim near Magdeburg is of
> interest, not only because it appears to have been one of the ear-
> liest appearances of the scourge in Germany, but because of the
> spate of superstitious beliefs and legends which surrounded the
> district for generations.
>
> The first victim was said to be the abbot of a Benedictine
> monastery, one Rudolph von Ginter, a man greatly hated in the
> district on account of his cruel and profligate life. His death met
> with general rejoicing, being considered a punishment from
> heaven, and bonfires were lit in the streets to celebrate it. Within
> weeks, however, the rest of the religious community and most
> of the local population followed him to the grave.

Marcus lit a cigarette as he turned over the leaf. The next page
was illustrated with a medieval woodcut, blurred and indistinct,
but it seemed to show a forest clearing at night with a thin moon
above the tree tops. In the foreground was the figure of a naked
man bent almost double beneath a wizened, ape-like being which
crouched upon his shoulders.

For more than three hundred years, the monastery ruins and grounds were regarded as an accursed place in which it was unsafe to venture, and a mass of legends surrounded them. These included the Black Virgin or Plague Maiden who rode upon the shoulders of a dead man, scattering dark red roses in her way, and a monstrous creature with the shape of a rat and the size of a wolf that stalked the area by night and on which it was death to look.

Marcus shook his head in disgust. 'Don't walk through the ruins, don't go near the park, For something pretty nasty may be waiting in the dark.' What the hell was he doing, poring over such rubbish? His place was at the microscope, not browsing through accounts of dead folklore. All the same, it must have been somewhere near Rudisheim that Billy Fenwick had vanished from the train. He read on.

These stories and fears persisted until the middle of the eighteenth century, when coal was discovered in the neighbourhood and Rudisheim grew into a small but fairly important industrial centre. In 1825 the Lutheran authorities bought part of the monastery grounds and built a church upon the site. While digging the foundations a bronze casting of a man's head was discovered and some scholars claim that it may have been taken from the death mask of the former abbot, Rudolph von Ginter. This relic was kept in the church as an historical curiosity till the end of the last war, when it disappeared.

A sickness of the soil, a miasma, a visitation from the stars against one evil man which destroyed a neighbourhood. Marcus put down the book and paced across the room. Was it possible that that was how it had happened? Could it have existed so long? Tiny spores lying dormant in dry soil or rubble till one day something disturbed them and a drop of moisture brought back normal reproduction?

And, after all, what were legends and superstitions? Childish nonsense, or warnings that had once been based on reality? Symbolic stories to protect simple people? Was there still a Plague

Maiden at Rudisheim? Could the sickness have lived on and something pretty nasty really be waiting in the dark? Marcus turned to the cages again. The big piebald rat was almost through the last barrier, but it looked very weak and there was a dribble of blood on its muzzle. He swung round as the door burst open.

'Hello, sir. Sorry to dash in like that, but I think you should see these at once.' Wilson laid a pile of morning papers on the table. 'It's making quite a stir.'

'Yes, quite a stir.' Marcus glanced at the first of them. Following last night's story, half the population of England appeared to think they might have been infected and hospitals had been deluged with demands for inoculation. In West Berlin, a laboratory had been broken into and a huge quantity of drugs stolen.

'Yes, I thought this might happen after those damned headlines,' he said. 'As always, you underestimate things, Peter.'

'Sorry, Sir Marcus, but you always used to say it was a good fault.' Wilson handed him a scribbled note. 'This came through to the switchboard just now. Another case in Berlin. The symptoms were about the same as the others.'

'Thanks.' Marcus held it under the light. 'Ruth Eulenburg – aged thirty-six – widow, living alone – no known connection with the Fenwick child established, but symptoms similar if not identical with those of Major Wood – found by police after telephone operator reported a woman sobbing and raving on the line – in ambulance kept repeating the name of somebody called Clever Gretel – died, seven a.m. Central European time.

'And she kept saying that, did she? Clever Gretel.' Marcus laid down the paper and looked at Wilson. 'Name mean anything to you, Peter?'

'Well, not really mean anything, sir. She was obviously just raving. I think Gretel is a fairy-story character. Maybe Hans Andersen.'

'No, it's Grimm, not Andersen. Gretel was the woman who kept planning against imaginary misfortunes. As you say, it probably was just delirious raving, but the Fenwick boy raved too. He kept talking about somebody named Iron Hans who is another character from Grimm. Don't you think there could be a connection?' He put his hand on Wilson's arm and stared hard at him.

'And tell me something else, Peter. We've been together a long time and I want the truth. This theory of mine, about a return of the Black Death bacillus: do you think there is anything in it, or am I going right round the bend?'

'No, sir, of course you're not. All the same, I do feel that it's too early to say what it is yet. I think you may be playing a hunch – jumping to conclusions without any –'

'Without any real evidence or proper observation.' Marcus picked up the newspaper again. 'You're quite right, of course, but what else can I do? We've no time for a full investigation. Once this thing gets going it could start the worst epidemic since the four-teenth century. I've just got to play my hunch and hope that it's right.' He glanced over his shoulder at the cages. The big rat had crawled into the top compartment where an ultra-violet bulb sim-ulated daylight, but it hadn't much longer to live. The blood from its jaw was a dark stream and it was staggering around in circles.

'Go and telephone General Kirk,' he said. 'The number is on my desk next door. Tell him I want a visa for East Germany straight away.' He stood watching the rat as Wilson hurried out of the room. It fell on its side kicking feebly, and he picked up his pad again.

'But who are they?' he thought, as he noted the time of the ani-mal's death. 'Who are they, and what is the connection? Iron Hans and Clever Gretel?'

*　*　*

Six hundred miles from the Central Laboratories another rat was dying. It wasn't a sleek, glossy specimen like Marcus Levin's, but an old, bloated grandfather of the sewers with warts around the ears and the scars of a hundred underground battles on its skin. It crawled slowly up from a man-made hole, twisted round three times like a kitten chasing its own tail and then fell on its side. In her little warm room a few yards away Clever Gretel was smiling.

Eleven

'This is Captain Hanks again, ladies and gentlemen, and once more I do apologize for having to ask you to keep your seat belts fastened a little longer.' The pilot's voice on the loudspeakers was breezy and self-assured. 'There's still a bit of bad weather in front of us, but nothing to be alarmed about. We're not going through it, but just taking a look-see, as one might say.' He chuckled but, as though in answer, the plane bucked violently and Kirk swayed across the seat, his shoulder colliding with Marcus Levin's.

'Sorry about that, ladies and gentlemen. My fault really. I should have kept above it, but I was hoping to get you to Tempelhof on time.'

'Why can't the fellow keep quiet and concentrate on flying his blasted aeroplane?' Kirk scowled and mopped his forehead. His face was an unhealthy, mottled green. 'On time indeed! We're fifteen minutes late already, and my appointment is for noon sharp.

'No, no, none of your pills, Doctor. I'm just going to bear it, though I can't say I feel like grinning.' He brushed aside Marcus's offer and turned to von Zuler, who had joined them at Hanover.

'And before I keep that appointment, Herr von Zuler, I must have more facts. This man Petrov has offered to see us personally, which proves, to my satisfaction at least, that the Russians are prepared to co-operate with us if we are able to give them certain assurances.' He tucked away his handkerchief and stared gloomily out of the port-hole at the swirling mist.

'But what assurance can I give them? What can I say to Petrov? We think that the Fenwick boy fell from the train somewhere between Magdeburg and the border. We think that he picked up the bug somewhere in East Germany and was smuggled into Berlin by one of the escape routes, but we can't prove anything. Since your people went and killed that sleeping-car attendant, we haven't even got one witness.'

70

'I know that, Herr General, and the officer responsible for Loser's death will stand trial for murder.' Von Zuler sat slumped far back in the seat with his metal leg stretched out in front of him. 'Whatever you say, though, I don't think we should presume that he was taken into West Berlin by one of the escape routes. At this stage we can't really be sure about anything.'

'No, we can't be sure, but in my mind there's very little doubt about it.' There was a sudden break in the cloud and through it Kirk could make out the line of the Berlin–Helmstedt autobahn. 'We know that that woman, Ruth Eulenburg, was a member of the Freiheit Organization which exists for the purpose of smuggling out refugees from the East. We know that she could have been infected by Billy Fenwick and, to me, it appears likely the name she kept repeating, Clever Gretel, was a code name for her contact in the East who brought the boy through. Doesn't that sound feasible to you?'

'Feasible, but not certain, General.' Von Zuler's eyes were half closed and he looked bored. 'At this stage, we just don't know what happened.'

'But we've damned well got to know.' Kirk's voice was very weary and his torn hand trembled on the arm of the seat. 'Sir Marcus has told you the seriousness of the situation and we have to find the original source before a full-scale epidemic breaks out. If it is in East Germany we must have the co-operation of the M.V.D., which means showing them that we have come in good faith. It could even mean giving them the names of the people who organize the escape routes. I'd hate to do that, but it may be necessary. You could supply me with those names, couldn't you, von Zuler?'

'I might be able to find them out for you, General Kirk, but at this stage I'm not even going to try.' The German stared across at him and his eyes were as hard as pebbles, screwed into his face by some revolting surgical operation.

'And would you really expect me to do so, General? To hunt down my own people and betray them to the Russians?'

'Yes, I may expect you to do that, Herr von Zuler. Believe me, I dislike the thought of it as much as you do, but to stop an epidemic it may be necessary.' Though Kirk felt sympathy for the man, it was quite unimportant as he remembered the things he had seen in the laboratory the night before.

'Sir Marcus,' he said, 'once again will you try and explain to Herr von Zuler just how serious this business is.'

'I'll try, General, but as I said before, I can't be very exact. At the moment we haven't got enough facts to be sure about anything.' Marcus turned to the German and heard himself automatically repeating the little that they did know: the production of the spores, the spread of the infection, the periods of incubation. As he spoke, the plane tilted slightly and he could see the city spread out beneath them; the Wannsee lakes like frosted glass, snow on the trees of the Grunewald and the tall mast of the Funkturm sliding away to the west. It was twenty years since he'd last seen it, and then he had been locked in a cattle-truck with fifty other human beings. He was more fortunate than most of his companions, though, for he'd been crammed against the side of the truck and through the slats he had looked out and seen a great glow in the sky. He'd felt hope for the first time in years as he watched that enormous light and known it was Berlin burning.

'This is Captain Hanks again, ladies and gentlemen.' The pilot's voice broke into his memories and explanation as the plane sank down to the rectangle of Tempelhof. 'We will be landing in a few moments, so please extinguish all cigarettes. I can't say that I hope you have had a pleasant trip after those bumps just now, but at least we are only twenty minutes behind schedule.'

'Thank you, Sir Marcus. That was a very clear explanation.' Von Zuler stubbed out his cigarette and nodded. 'I am sure the situation could become as serious as you say, but I haven't changed my mind yet.

'No, gentlemen, though this disease may be all you claim, there have only been three reported cases so far, and that's not enough to make me do what you ask.' His hard eyes were pleading as he looked across at Kirk.

'As an Englishman, General, you can't understand what those escape routes mean to us in Germany. Since the wall went up, only a trickle of people manage to get through, of course, but at least there is a trickle. At least there is some hope that families may be reunited one day. Without them I think we might have a mass hysteria, a group neurosis on our hands which would make your plague epidemic appear almost unimportant. It is likely that their chief organizer is somebody in the East German hierarchy who risks his life every minute just to help others. I don't know his name and I wouldn't tell you if I did. No, Sir Marcus, unless the medical authorities can give me more proof of the dangers involved, I just can't help you.'

'We will, Herr von Zuler. We'll give you the proof all right, or rather that bacillus will. God, can't you realize the speed at which it can spread?' As he spoke a clear picture of the things floating on the slide, dividing and releasing their spores, flashed through Marcus's mind. 'There may be only three reported cases so far, but how many others are there which we don't know about? Can't you try and imagine what will happen once it really breaks out in a big city? We were lucky to get the boy's contacts, but . . .'

'Easy, Doctor. Just take it easy.' Kirk's hand gripped his arm and cut short the outburst. Already the plane had touched down and was running towards the reception building. Marcus nodded wearily and picked up his case, praying for a miracle to change the German's mind.

'Zu Befehl, Herr Kommissar.' One of von Zuler's assistants was waiting on the tarmac. He clicked his heels and bowed stiffly to Kirk and Marcus, obviously impressed by a full general and an internationally known specialist. A porter and two uniformed policemen were standing beside him.

'A car is waiting, gentlemen, and arrangements have been made for you to pass through the Brandenburger check point into East Berlin. But I was asked to give this to Sir Marcus Levin. It is from Professor Mannheim of the Semmelweiss Hospital.'

'Thank you.' Marcus ripped open the envelope. Mannheim's observations were almost exactly the same as his own. Abnormal sporification, abnormal reproductivity, abnormal speed in the life cycle. And so far no antibiotic or bacteriocide to touch it. Everything they knew and dreaded and not one ray of hope. He stuffed the letter into his pocket, preparing to follow Kirk and von Zuler to the reception hall, and then paused. The porter was coming down the steps with their bags now. A heavy, middle-aged man in a faded blue uniform, with a face which was remarkable for nothing except stupidity. But as he looked at his face, Marcus had the strange feeling that he should know him, that he had seen him somewhere before, that it was important that he remembered where.

Yes, the face really was familiar. Thick, stupid features bloated with cold, a curved nose and a double chin which pressed against the folds of his jacket as he lifted the bags on to the trolley. Just where had he seen the man?

'Aren't you coming, old boy?' Kirk frowned back at him. 'Do let's hurry up and get inside. It's freezing out here.'

'Yes, of course. I'm just coming.' Marcus followed him towards the entrance. It was ridiculous, of course. Though he'd never been to Tempelhof before, there could be a dozen explanations. The man obviously resembled someone else or had worked at an airport in West Germany. Hamburg perhaps. He'd been to Hamburg himself three times last year. Yes, that was probably it, and you really must control yourself, he thought. Already his hunch about Rudisheim felt slightly ridiculous, and now this. Anxiety because a porter's face looked familiar.

All the same, it was important. Something told him that it was important. He stopped and turned. The porter was coming up the slope toward him, and though he looked strong enough, he was making heavy weather of it; the barrow zigzagging on the concrete and his breath like a cloud of steam in the cold air. He had to remember where he had seen that face before. A hooked nose between swollen cheeks, bloodshot brown eyes and a heavy double chin straining against the uniform jacket. And then as he watched him Marcus knew that he had been wrong: he had never seen the man before. It was what had happened to him that he recognized. The features couldn't have been merely bloated with cold because the cheeks were so swollen as to appear flat and the jaw was twice its normal size. 'Lion-faced' was the usual way of describing the condition, and the last time he had seen it was shortly before Billy Fenwick died.

'Just a minute, porter. Please put down your barrow for a moment. I am a doctor and I want to ask you something.' Marcus nodded as the man lowered the shafts and stared vacantly at him. His breath was stale and sour and he drew back slightly before it. Was he really safe, he wondered? Could he be sure that the vaccine had taken?

'Anything wrong, Sir Marcus? One of your cases been left behind?' Von Zuler came hurrying back to him, but he waved him aside.

'No, nothing like that, but keep away from us please. And get somebody on to the Isolation Hospital. Have them send over an ambulance right away.

'Now, porter, please sit down on the bench over here and let me look at you. Good.' The man's forehead felt like a hot-water bottle under his fingers and the pulse was racing. 'What is your name?'

'Kubisiac. Franz Kubisiac.'

'Well, don't worry, Franz. Everything is going to be all right.' Even in the bare concrete corridor the smooth, bedside manner came automatically to him. 'How long have you been feeling ill?'

'About two days, Herr Doktor, but it is nothing.' The man shook his head stupidly. 'Only a little chill that will soon pass. Now, please let me get on with my work, Herr Doktor.'

'In a moment, Franz, in just a moment, but first I want to ask you something else. Were you on duty when the little English boy was put on the plane? Did you go near him?'

'Yes, but what if I did? What has that to do with it? As I told you, this is just a chill and I want to get on with my work.' There was anger as well as stupidity in his eyes now.

'I see, just a chill, eh? And you didn't get yourself inoculated, Franz? You knew that you should have done, but you were afraid your arm would swell up and you would lose overtime perhaps? Have you a family to keep?' Marcus's hand reached out towards the tunic as he spoke.

'Yes, a wife and three kids; little girls. They need a lot of money. All the time my wife asks for money. I couldn't afford to go sick. Now, please let me get on, Herr Doktor.'

'No, Franz, not till I've had a proper look at you. But keep those people away, can't you?' Quite a crowd was beginning to gather in the passage and Marcus motioned von Zuler to hold them back.

'And now let me have a look at your chest, Franz. It won't take a moment.' His fingers were undoing the top button when Kubisiac's face altered. A second before it had merely shown stupidity and anger but without any warning it suddenly changed to a mask of almost animal rage. 'No,' he said. 'No, no, leave me alone!' He stood up, his body stiffened, and his arm swung out like a flail. 'Just leave me alone!'

'Stop him! Don't let him get away!' It felt as though the Adam's apple had been torn out of his throat, but even as he fell Marcus tried to make them understand. Typical, he thought, feeling his knees start to buckle and his umbrella snap under his weight. As with rats the will to escape is the only emotion which remains important. Quite typical. The concrete floor rushed up to meet him and the world went dark.

'You all right, Doctor?' They had propped him on the bench and Kirk's face was frowning down at him. 'Feeling better?'

'Yes, I'm all right.' His eyes seemed to blur for a moment and then steady themselves into focus. 'How long have I been out? Only a few seconds? Good. And the porter, Kubisiac? You stopped him?'

'Yes, after he went berserk and hit you, one of the policemen laid him out with his truncheon. They put him in a waiting room over there. But take it easy, old boy. Sit still for a bit. It was a hell of a bang he gave you.' Kirk's eyes were full of concern as Marcus stood up and moved towards the room.

'No, I'm all right. Quite all right, but I must look at him.' He steadied himself against the door frame as the floor seemed to tilt slightly, and walked on. Kubisiac was lying on a sofa by the far wall, and there was a mirror above him. Marcus grinned ruefully back at it. Sir Marcus Levin the natty dresser, he thought. Marcus Levin who takes such a pride in his appearance. Well, you don't look very natty now. Blood was dripping on to his collar from a graze on his cheek, his jacket was covered with white dust and his right eye was starting to blacken. He shrugged his shoulders and then bent down over Kubisiac. The man's eyes were open but he was quite unconscious.

'And I don't want anybody in here till the ambulance arrives,' he said, and then changed his mind, remembering the miracle he had prayed for on the plane. 'That is, nobody except you, Herr von Zuler. I would like you to see this, please.' He watched von Zuler come towards him and ripped open Kubisiac's tunic and shirt. In the V of the sweat-stained vest was the thing he knew he would find: the scarlet rash like tiny roses on the skin.

'Herr von Zuler,' he said. 'A few minutes ago you refused to give General Kirk the information he needs till you have more proof of the dangers involved.

'Well, here is your proof. This man was infected because for a short space of time he breathed the same air as the Fenwick boy. He will probably die and he has a wife and three children who are almost certainly carriers by now.' He gripped the German's arm and pulled him forward.

'Go on, look at him, von Zuler. Smell his breath, examine the rash, better still feel his body.' His free hand undid Kubisiac's trouser buttons as he spoke.

'Yes, that's it. Put your hand into the groin and tell me that you need more proof.' Von Zuler was struggling against him but Levin forced his arm down.

'Yes, you can feel the bubo, can't you? Be very careful because it could burst at any moment. About the size of a small plum, would you say? It's hard and corrugated too though, isn't it? Perhaps rather like a walnut? Go on, make a proper examination, and then tell me that you still refuse the information.'

'Please, please, Sir Marcus.' Von Zuler's body went suddenly slack and then with a single, convulsive jerk he pulled himself free and stood staring at Marcus. He didn't seem able to speak for a moment and his eyes didn't look completely sane.

'All right,' he said, when at last he could say anything. 'All right. You win. I'll get you the names you want and may God forgive me for it.' He turned and lurched out into the corridor, fighting to control his urge to vomit.

Twelve

'Ah, there you are at last, gentlemen. Better late than never, and it is a great pleasure to welcome you here.' Gregor Petrov jumped up from behind a desk, bowed, smiled and stretched out his hand, apparently in a single action. He was dressed in what he hoped would impress Kirk as being the best possible taste: corduroy slacks and a thick green Harris tweed jacket purchased in London fifteen years ago. On his little pudgy body they gave him the air of a forest gnome waiting to ensnare the lost traveller in some rather sinister fairy story.

'General Kirk,' he said, beaming up at him and squeezing his hand. 'General Charles Kirk, my old antagonist in person. Walk into my parlour, General. I shall regard this meeting as one of the high-spots of my life.' He chuckled and turned to Marcus, his three chins joggling up and down over his tight collar.

'And you, sir, will be Sir Marcus Levin. A pleasure, too, though I am sorry to hear of your unfortunate experience at the airport. Oh, yes, General, we also have our sources of information.'

'But let me introduce you to my colleagues. Colonel Gustav Behr of the People's Police; Dr Glauser from the Potsdam Institute of Histopathology who has kindly offered to help us; my secretary, Miss Tania Valina. Would you do the honours, please, Tania?'

He nodded approvingly as the girl brought over a tray of glasses.

'Good. Now, let's sit down and be comfortable, gentlemen. Take this chair by the fire, General. I have heard of your dislike of badly-heated rooms and only hope that this one is warm enough. I had it specially built up for you.' The stove was almost red-hot and looked big enough to propel a small ship.

'It is most comfortable, Comrade Petrov.' Kirk studied him as he smiled back. He knew that Petrov, for all his benevolent, slightly comic manner, was a very shrewd man who would drive a hard bargain before giving any co-operation.

'Excellent. But please don't call me "Comrade", General Kirk. It

is a rather archaic form of address now, only used by our real die-
hards; my wife amongst them. I would much prefer "Mister".

'Be careful, though, General. Be very careful which glass you
take.' He chuckled again as Tania held out the tray. 'Four glasses
contain nothing but good Russian vodka, but perhaps the other
two may have been doctored. Sorry, Sir Marcus.' He grinned apolo-
getically, congratulating himself on his colloquial English.

'Perhaps when you drink from them you will both sleep a little.
And, while he is sleeping, General Kirk might be persuaded to tell
me some very interesting things about his organization. What
would you use to make him talk, Sir Marcus? Pentothal perhaps?'

'I'll take a chance on that, Mr Petrov. Thank you.' Kirk picked
up the nearest glass. 'I don't think the details of either of our organizations are of much importance at the moment, except in so
far as they can help us to locate the source of this plague. And, if
they can't locate it quickly, I think we may be both out of business
before long.'

'I see. Then your very good health, gentlemen. Your good
health and to the destruction of this mysterious disease of which
I have heard so much and "do in part believe", if I may quote from
Shakespeare.' He raised his glass and knocked back the vodka in a
single quick movement.

'Now, let's get down to business, shall we?' He replaced the glass
on the tray and stopped smiling. As he did so his face lost all its
benevolent flabbiness.

'I have naturally seen your newspapers and listened to your
radio, General. I have also read through the very full account you
sent us and heard what our own agents in England and West Germany have been able to find out. I'm afraid that I still only do in
part believe.' His hand rapped sharply on the table as though swat-
ting a fly he had seen crawling across it and he turned to Marcus
Levin.

'Sir Marcus,' he said, 'I understand that you have brought the
technical data of this – this scourge with you. As they will probably
be incomprehensible to all of us except Dr Glauser, perhaps you
would take them over to the desk there and go through them with
him. Thank you.'

Petrov watched the two men move away and then looked past them out of the window. The snow was still swirling over the Linden. Clean, cold snow, blanketing the earth and purifying it. He believed every word in Kirk's report, but he wasn't going to admit it; not yet. Though he could die of plague as easily as anyone else, though he dreaded the very thought of an epidemic, it was still his job to exploit the situation.

'Well, General, let's have all the facts. Let's have all your cards on the table. I am prepared to believe that this disease is as deadly and repulsive as your report states, and I agree that we must co-operate with you in finding the source and wiping it out. But . . .' Once more his hand rapped the table. 'Just where is that source, General?

'Oh, yes, I know what you people say. That the child fell from a train which was passing through East Germany and he became infected here. But what evidence can you give us that this is true? Remember that your earlier story stated that we had kidnapped the boy to bring pressure on his father who worked in some signals office. Not a very charitable idea, General, and the present version is scarcely more so. Look for yourself.' He picked up a copy of the *Morning Echo* and handed it to Kirk. The headlines read 'Russian Germs Loose', and a notice at the foot of the column urged the reader to turn to John Forest's report on page 2.

'No, not very friendly, is it? We are accused of running some kind of bacteriological warfare establishment in Germany, letting a culture get loose by accident and then rounding up all infected persons to pretend there has been no outbreak over here.'

'That is not the official view, Mr Petrov, and there will be no more articles of this kind.' Kirk scowled at the page. 'Orders for censorship have already been given.'

'I am sure they have, my friend. Just as we have given orders to stop this.' Petrov tapped a copy of *Pravda*. 'I don't know if you read Russian, but this is the same sort of thing, except that the parts are reversed. Here it says that the germs came from a Western establishment, the Fenwick child was never in East Germany at all, and the whole business is a trick to discredit the peace-loving Soviet people. "Jackals", "spreaders of filth" are some of the terms used to describe you.' He pushed the paper away from him, as though it were an extremely disgusting object.

'Yes, lies, General. I am personally sure of that. But can you prove they are lies, any more than we can disprove what your Press says about us? Our medical experts seem to be falling foul of each other, though.' The two doctors were arguing violently. Glauser's face was flushed and Marcus appeared to be regarding him with a look of bored contempt: the expression of a man who could make an apology sound far worse than his original insult.

'And let's have the East German view. Colonel Behr, will you please tell the general what your people have discovered so far?'

'There is nothing to tell – nothing at all.' Behr was a tall, thin man with a rather sour and old-maidish expression. He looked more like a schoolteacher than a policeman. 'A most thorough investigation was made and there have been no cases of plague reported any-where in our territory. Nor is there the slightest evidence that the child was ever in the People's Republic. In my opinion the *Pravda* article is materially correct. If the bacillus exists, it must have come from the West.'

'Thank you, Gustav.' Petrov leaned back in his chair and nodded. 'There you are, General Kirk. There has been no outbreak here, so why should we co-operate with you?'

'Because you can die of plague as well as we can, Mr Petrov, and I don't think your wall will keep it out.' Kirk turned away from him and looked at Behr. He had never felt more miserable in his life. Von Zuler had kept his word to Marcus. Half an hour after arriv-ing at Tempelhof he had got them the information they needed to bargain with Petrov. Kirk hated the thought of giving it to him, but now he knew that he would have to.

'Yes, we can die of plague, General.' As though reading his mind, the Russian smiled again. 'And you will get the collaboration you ask for. If the source of this germ is in East Germany, it will be found. I will also allow Sir Marcus to go anywhere he wants and provide him with an escort. In return you must collaborate with me. The boy can only have reached West Berlin by one of the es-cape routes, and to trace his movements we must talk to the people who brought him through. Well, where can we find them, General Kirk? Who is Brother Lustig?'

Brother Lustig? Kirk's head jerked back in his surprise. Von Zuler hadn't mentioned the code name, but it was all fitting together. Another character from Grimm: the soldier who gave away his last crust to a beggar. Iron Hans, Clever Gretel, and now Brother Lustig.

'This is ridiculous, Gregor.' Behr broke in before he could answer. There was an odd expression on his face which Kirk couldn't recognize, though he felt he should know what it was. 'Brother Lustig is dead. He was killed in Heinersdorf six months ago while trying to escape from the police. His real name was Gunter Kirsten and since he died we have closed all the escape routes. You have my word for that, Gregor. No refugees get out today and the whole story is a Western trick to discredit us; a propaganda stunt. Lustig is dead.'

'So you have told me, Gustav; many times.' Petrov stood up and massaged his hands over the stove. 'And once again I repeat that I don't believe you. I think that you are trying to pretend to yourself that your department is rather more efficient than it really is.

'No, Kirsten wasn't Brother Lustig, Gustav. The man, or possibly woman, is still alive. I know it. I can feel it. Somebody we trust probably. Somebody in authority who has fooled us for years. And we are going to get him, Gustav. We are going to get him and we are going to make him talk. When he talks, not only will the escape routes be finished for good and all, but their organizers will be in the hollow of my hand.' He held out his right hand, grinning at it, and nodded to Kirk.

'After that, General, you will not have to worry about me any more. I shall retire, loaded down with honours. Who knows, they might even give me an Order of Lenin? Stranger things have happened.'

'Mr Petrov, it is five o'clock. Time for the British news.' Tania had already got up and crossed to the radio.

'Yes, turn it on, my dear. I expect that our friends will like to hear the recent developments from their country.' Petrov sat down again as the announcer's voice echoed across the room.

'. . . three further cases of bubonic plague have been reported in

London this morning and the government is expected to announce a national emergency at any moment. The Queen and the Duke of Edinburgh are returning from Sandringham tonight. At North Kensington this afternoon a number of people were detained when rioting broke out at an immunization centre. The trouble appears to have started when three men attempted to force their way to the front of a queue. In the ensuing struggle a seventeen-year-old youth received severe head injuries. Replying to Mr Dylan Mogg-Rees for the Opposition, the Minister of Health stated that ample stocks of serum were available and there was no undue cause for alarm.'

'You have heard enough, General?' Petrov motioned to Tania to switch off the set.

'Yes, things begin to move, don't they?' More cases, civil disturbance, a national emergency, your Royal Family hurrying home to show that all is well. Doesn't that prove that you must collaborate with us now? If we are to help you must tell us how that boy entered West Berlin.' His eyes were quite unblinking as he stared at Kirk.

'Come on, General, I'm waiting. Who is Brother Lustig?'

'Gregor Ilyavitch, this is ridiculous.' Behr leaned forward, shaking his head. 'There is no such person any more. Lustig is dead. He was killed in Heinersdorf, as I told you.'

'Shut up, Gustav.' Without taking his eyes from Kirk, the Russian turned slightly towards the men at the desk. 'Well, gentlemen, you have had some minutes of discussion. Are you agreed about the seriousness of the situation?'

'We are agreed in part, Comrade Petrov.' Marcus Levin had obviously got the better of the argument and Glauser sounded slightly crushed. 'I still consider that this bacillus is a man-made mutant, probably produced in the West. I do agree, however, that unless we can find the source soon and also an effective bacteriocide, the world is in very great danger.'

'Thank you, Doctor.' Petrov's hand tapped up and down on the desk as he spoke. 'Well, General Kirk, it's up to you, isn't it? Only you can help us to find the source. How did the Fenwick boy enter West Berlin? Who is Brother Lustig?'

'Give me a minute, Mr Petrov. Just one minute.' Kirk looked away from him and stared at the stove. He could see a row of faces melting before it and all of them were his own. Had it been the same with other betrayers, he wondered? Had Judas felt hell fire as he took the silver? In a few seconds he would have to kill the hopes of half a nation and destroy a man for whom he felt deep respect. There was nothing else that he could do. 'National Emergency' – 'More Cases' – 'Civil Disturbance'. Four short sentences on the radio had destroyed all freedom of choice.

'Yes, I'll tell you,' he said at last, but he was speaking to Behr rather than Petrov. The German looked completely bored and indifferent, the observer of some dull and badly acted play longing for the final curtain.

'The man you want – the man who runs the escape routes and calls himself Brother Lustig is . . . No . . .' His voice became a shout and he jumped to his feet. 'No, don't do it. You mustn't do it.' He hurled himself across the table, but he was too late. Slowly and indifferently, as though the action was completely trivial, Gustav Behr pulled out a revolver, placed the muzzle in his mouth and pressed the trigger.

Thirteen

A fool's errand, a wild-goose chase, a labour in vain. The phrases ran through Marcus Levin's head against the clatter of the car chains. What the hell, he thought, just what the hell are you doing and what do you expect to find? Fairy tales, legends, the history of a monastery that has been deserted for six hundred years. While at every minute, in every news bulletin, more cases were being reported and the pandemic was gathering strength.

All the same, though he couldn't explain why, Marcus knew that he was right in going to Rudisheim. He lit a cigarette and stared out through the windscreen. The wipers were having a struggle to keep it clear and the snow swirled and eddied across the flat countryside, though to the left of the road he could make out a railway embankment. The same line, possibly, along which his cattle-truck had rumbled to Belsen so many years ago. In the rich, crowded streets of West Germany he was always conscious of that journey, but today, driving through the untilled fields and broken-down villages of the East, it seemed strangely unimportant, almost as though it had happened to someone else.

'Can I give you a spell, my dear?' He looked across at Tania Valina. 'You have been driving a long time now.'

'It is all right. I enjoy it. Besides I do not suppose your licence will be valid for what they call Iron Curtain countries.' She smiled at him without taking her eyes off the road. 'You speak very good Russian, Sir Marcus.'

'Thank you. It is a long time since I had the opportunity to do so.' He nodded, trying to remember just how many languages he did know. Two classical, four European, Yiddish, Hindi and three Oriental dialects which she wouldn't have heard of.

'But tell me something. Why did Mr Petrov supply you as my escort? Was he merely being courteous, or did he want somebody he trusts to keep an eye on my movements? To see that I don't get up to any mischief?'

'Both, Sir Marcus. You want to go to this place Rudisheim as a private person . . . to question the inhabitants without appearing to have any official position. Mr Petrov thought I would be an unobtrusive escort and also carry a certain authority should you come up against the East German authorities.' She grinned to herself, remembering Petrov's actual words. 'This man is said to be a great medical expert, but in other matters he may be a fool. It is up to you to see that he neither makes, nor gets into, any trouble. To be a little mother to him, in fact.'

'And do you think that Colonel Behr will die, Sir Marcus?'

'He'll die all right. He's probably dead already.' Marcus glanced at the dashboard clock. It was over two and a half hours since Behr had pulled out his revolver. 'If General Kirk hadn't managed to knock his hand to one side he would have died on the spot. The question is, can they make him talk before he dies?' That was ludicrous, of course. The word was communicate, for Behr would never talk again. The blast and the bullet had shattered his vocal cords and torn the tongue to shreds. He had somehow retained con-

sciousness, though. Marcus remembered how the man had struggled against Glauser and himself as they fought to save his life. By
some trick of extra-sensory perception he had almost seemed to
hear him praying for their fingers to slip from the arteries and let
the blood drain away.

Nonsense, too! There was no such thing as telepathy; no scientific proof for it. It was as absurd as . . . Yes, as absurd as his own
hunch – the wild-goose chase which was taking them to Rudisheim.

'But he must talk. They must make him tell everything before
he dies.' As though to drive home the point, Tania accelerated and
the car took the next bend like a sledge. 'They must make him
tell everything. Not only about the English boy, but about the escape routes and the people he worked with. To think that during all
those years he worked for the Vopo he was betraying us.'

'Yes, I suppose he was a traitor, and I agree that, if it is possible,
he must give up his information. But don't you think he was quite
a patriot as well? He gambled his life every minute of the day and,
when he was finally found out, he tried to kill himself rather than
expose his comrades. Can't you appreciate that, Miss Valina?'

'I can appreciate nothing about such creatures.' Another bend
loomed ahead and once again her foot came down on the accelerator. 'To me they are just vermin.'

'I see. You are a hard woman, I'm afraid, comrade.' Marcus
pulled at his cigarette and then clutched the door handle as the car
corkscrewed across the road, narrowly missing a telegraph pole.
'Look out, though. You'll have us over in a minute.'

'It is all right. I am a good driver and this is a very safe car; a
lovely car.' She beamed proprietorially at the bonnet of the battered Zis. 'Do you have a car of your own in England, Sir Marcus?'

'Yes, I have a car.' An image of his gleaming Ferrari shone before
Marcus's eyes. 'A much nicer car than this, Comrade Valina.'

'I see. Then you are either a braggart or a very rich man. Both
bad things, I think. Yes, Sir Marcus Levin, the rich English Jew.'

'Quite right. I'm rich enough. Do you object to my being a Jew?'

'Do I object?' Tania frowned slightly. 'On the question of the
Semitic problem, I naturally follow the Party line. As far as I have
any personal views on the subject . . .' Her frown deepened in con-

centration. 'Mr Petrov has a thing about his staff speaking colloquial English and I took a course last year. Let me see if I can
express myself in it.' She took her eyes off the road for a moment
and glanced across at him.

'No, Sir Marcus, I don't give a damn about your being a Jew,
one way or the other. At the same time, I have been told that all
Western Jews are rich.'

'Then, if I may reply in a similar manner, you've been fed a load
of crap, my sweet.' Marcus laughed and relaxed as the car finally
reached a straight stretch of road. 'Oh, Luba,' he said, humming
lightly against the whine of the engine. 'Oh, Luba, my little Bol-
shevik girl.'

'My name is Tania.' She frowned again and then smiled. 'Oh, I
see. You know that song, Sir Marcus? About the woman who hangs
about army camps. Where did you hear it?'

'A long, long time ago, my dear. Probably before you were born.'
Marcus considered how it had been. The Soviet troops had looked
as though they would stay in the town indefinitely, and then one
day they had marched out and an S.S. regiment moved in.

'I heard it in Poland during the spring of '40,' he said. 'Let me see
if I can remember the words. Yes, "Though your body's like a hay
sack and you're barmy, it's your vigour makes us shrug aside the
cost. You're the backbone of our mighty Russian army. Without
you the Bolsheviki – Without you the Bolsheviki – ".' Marcus waved
his cigarette like a baton and Tania joined him in a rich, throbbing
contralto. ' "Without you the Bolsheviki would be lost . . . ".'

The car clattered over a wooden bridge, lurched up a slope and
slid past a sign that read 'Rudisheim 16 Km.'

* * *

'In an hour, comrade, maybe two, even in a few minutes. Who
knows?' The doctor straightened from the operating table. Above
the wad of bandages around his neck, Behr looked as though he
were already dead, and tubes ran from jars and cylinders into his
body.

'If you ask me, it is a wonder that he is still alive. Without oxygen and the constant transfusions he would have gone out a long time ago.'

'Yes, so you have said before.' Petrov nodded. 'But before he dies, is there any chance that he can be made to talk? He has certain information which it is essential . . .'

'Talk?' The doctor smiled at all lay ignorance. 'There is not the slightest chance of his talking, Comrade Petrov. The vocal cords are shattered and we had to remove most of his tongue before we could stop the bleeding. Even if he wished to talk – even if we pumped him full of EX3, it would be impossible. And this man doesn't want to talk.' He leaned forward over Behr again and shook his head. 'He just wants to die.'

EX3. Kirk pricked up his ears with professional interest. So that was the name of their latest truth drug, was it? Poor devil, though. Behr's eyes were open and they seemed to be pleading for death. Pleading to be able to protect his organization and the names of the people who had worked with him. He felt great compassion as he looked at him.

All the same, they had to make him communicate somehow. They had to trace Billy Fenwick's movements right back to the time he fell from the train. Somewhere along his route he must have picked up the disease and they had to find all his contacts: Iron Hans and Clever Gretel and whoever else had helped him. On the last news flash more cases had been reported; four in London and three in Western Germany. Seven bodies growing black, with the rash like a ring of tiny red flowers on the chest, and the obscene things between the thighs pulsing as though they had a life of their own.

And soon there would be more cases – soon the epidemic would start to spiral. The vaccine appeared to be working all right, but how long would stocks last? Less than an hour ago a Hanover doctor had been almost beaten to death because he had run out of serum. Once infection had taken place there was no drug to help, either, and public confidence would be breaking down before long. They had to find the source, the first carrier, and, though Marcus Levin might have gone off to Rudisheim following his hunch, Kirk was quite sure that Behr was the only person who could help them.

Somehow he had to be made to give up his information.

'Excuse me a moment, Doctor,' he said. 'You have made it very clear to us that the man is unable to talk, but you also said that the spinal column is undamaged and there is a motor connection between the brain and the rest of the body. Now, if he wanted to communicate, is it possible that he might be able to write down the answers to a few simple questions?'

'Write!' It was Kirk's turn to receive that pitying smile. 'This man is practically dead already, Herr General. He is under maximum stimulation. You might just as well expect him to get up and walk across the room. Look for yourself.' He took a probe from the tray and held it between Behr's fingers. As soon as he removed his hand they opened and it fell to the floor.

'You see, Herr General?'

'Yes, I see, Doctor. I think that I really do see at last.' Kirk felt a sudden gleam of hope as he looked at Behr. For the last two hours the man's body had lain quite motionless, but now he had moved. For perhaps five seconds after the probe had fallen his right index finger had tapped against the side of the table.

'Gregor Ilyavitch,' he said, turning to Petrov. They had dropped formality from the moment that Behr shot himself. 'Did you notice the way his finger moved just now? As a policeman he will probably know the Morse code, and if he is able to move his fingers, he might . . .'

'Yes, yes, I understand. That could be our way.' Petrov frowned for a second and then his little pudgy hand squeezed Kirk's arm. 'Good, very good indeed. You are a clever fellow, my friend.' He turned to an assistant standing by the door. 'Get over to headquarters and bring back a buzzer and a couple of Morse keys. Be as quick as you can about it.

'Now, Doctor,' he said. 'Just what will happen if you give him this stuff of yours; the EX3? Will it make him want to communicate with us, even though he is unable to do so?'

'It will make him want to do anything you ask, Comrade Petrov, but he is so weak that . . .' He felt Behr's pulse and shrugged his shoulders.

'EX3 is a variant of Psilocybin administered with an accelerator.

It has been used in the treatment of certain mental disturbances for years, but only recently has your profession adopted it.

'The general effect is to take the subject right back into the past so that he remembers things which have been shut away for years: childhood terrors of the dark, the feel of his mother's nipple, even what it was like to be a foetus in the womb. All that is re-lived in a matter of minutes, and afterwards he will feel so free, so contented and cleansed that he will want to answer any question you put to him. All the same, I don't think we should give him an injection. In his condition the initial shock will quite probably kill him.'

'Don't worry about that, Doctor. I will take full responsibility. You said he is dying anyway, so we have nothing to lose.' Petrov stared down at Behr's face. And I trusted you, Gustav, he thought. For years I trusted you. I almost counted you a friend, while all the time, right under our noses, you were betraying us. But now you are going to talk to me, Gustav. It will be the last action of your life, but you are going to tell me everything.

'And how long after the injection shall we know if he has stood up to this initial shock, Doctor?

'I see. Ten to fifteen minutes. Then give it to him. As I said, the responsibility is mine.' He watched him start to fill a syringe and turned to Kirk.

'Well, General,' he said, 'let's hope that your idea works. I don't know if you are a religious man, but if you are, I would advise you to pray. As a good dialectical materialist I am supposed to deny the existence of a personal God, but at this moment I am rather inclined to join you.' The drug had been administered now and they both glanced up at the big electric clock on the wall. One minute – two – three, and no change at all. Four – five; Behr's left eyelid quivered slightly, but nothing else happened. Six – seven; a little spasm of pain flickered across his face and he groaned. Eight – nine; his face became quite rigid for a moment with the eyes opening wider and wider till they seemed to be bursting out from the sockets. Ten – eleven – twelve, his whole body went slack and the eyes closed. The doctor reached out for the pulse again.

'He's made it, comrade,' he said. 'He's all yours, but I've not the slightest idea how long he will last.'

'Thank you. Yes, give them to me please.' Petrov's assistant had returned and he took the equipment from him.

'Now, just stand to one side, Doctor. You've done all that was required of you.' He pulled up a chair beside the table, laid the buzzer beside Behr's head and very gently placed his finger on the Morse key. 'I imagine that it will be better if I try to contact him in Morse. In that way the reflexes might help.

'Well, are you still praying?' He grinned at Kirk as he lifted the other key. 'I very much doubt if this will work, but it appears to be our only chance.

'Der der dot – dot dot der – dot dot dot – der . . .' The tinny sound of the buzzer rang across the room. 'Gustav, you must tell me everything. How did the child reach West Berlin? Who are the people who brought him through? Dot dot dot dot – dot der – der dot – dot dot dot. Who is Hans, Gustav? Who are Iron Hans and Clever Gretel?'

Fourteen

'There is no truth in it whatsoever.' For the fifth time Sergeant Goltz of the Rudisheim police bellowed the denial. He and his attendant minion, Constable Braun, were two vast men filled with self-esteem and, judging by their breath, several glasses of schnapps. Bearded and suitably dressed they could have brought down the house as pantomime ogres, and Marcus would have been only mildly surprised if Goltz had exclaimed 'Fe fo fi fum,' instead of 'Papiere bitte,' as he demanded their passports.

But, however great their self-importance, Tania's credentials had brought them to heel with much bowing and scraping and 'Gnä'es Fräuleins' and 'Zu Befehl, Herr Doktors'. Once it was established that she and Marcus had not come for any sinister motive, such as inspecting the police station, the giants' hospitality knew no bounds. Chairs had been pulled up before the stove in a small, private office, a bottle of cheap 'Clara' was produced and the fortunes of the Soviet Union, Great Britain, and the People's Republic of East Germany solemnly toasted. After Marcus's first question, however, helpfulness had ended abruptly.

'No, no, no.' Goltz was obviously incapable of normal speech and he shouted at the top of his voice, pacing across the floor with his huge face set in a scowl of disbelief. 'No, no, no.' The boards shuddered beneath his feet and Marcus could almost hear the thud of the big drum as the giant lumbered on to the stage.

'No, it is impossible. How often must I repeat that it is impossible?' His blue tunic was wrinkled and crumpled as if it could scarcely contain the enormous chest, and below it his stomach stood out like the broad end of a pear.

'For three days, Fräulein. For three days and nights people have done nothing but ask questions about that English child and I am getting sick and tired of it. We have had the army searching the district. Berlin has been on the telephone almost every hour. Even Major Fischer from Magdeburg has been over to see us. And I have told them all that it is just not possible that the boy could have been here.' He came heavily to rest by the table and knocked back another glass of schnapps.

'Comrade Valina, this is my town. Before the war ten thousand people lived here. Now there are less than three thousand and I know them all. I was born here and I know every house and bomb site and rat-hole in Rudisheim. Is it possible that the boy could have been harboured here and I not have known about it?' He swung round to his subordinate for confirmation. 'Comrade Braun, is it possible?'

'It is quite impossible, Comrade Goltz.' The constable nodded in agreement. If anything he was slightly bigger than his superior and a deep scar on his right cheek gave his face a rather sinister and vulpine expression.

'Our investigations have been most thorough, and in my opinion the child never existed at all. The whole story is just a fabrication; propaganda put out by certain parties to discredit the Republic.' He glowered up at the wall above the stove. It was decorated by a photograph of Mr Mikoyan smiling at a small blond child who had just presented him with a bunch of flowers. Beside Mikoyan was a poster showing a simian creature dressed in American uniform with a rope around its hairy neck. 'We have enough trees in East Berlin to hang every Western war-monger,' read the caption beneath it.

'Do you agree with me, Comrade Goltz?'

'I agree with you entirely, Comrade Braun; all propaganda.' His glass crashed down on the table to emphasize the point. Now that the initial shock of seeing Tania's credentials had worn off, the giants were getting out of hand. They had obviously run the town without check or interference for years, probably making a very good thing out of it, and the recent attention from outside was a sore point with them.

'Yes, propaganda. Dirty Western propaganda.' Again his glass beat on the table and again Marcus seemed to hear the thud of a drum from the orchestra pit. At any moment Goltz would declare that he smelt 'the blood of an Englishmun'. He turned away from the glowering face and studied the pictures on the wall. The photograph looked oddly pitted and pockmarked, as though breaking out in a rash, and it only took him seconds to see why. Goltz and Braun might rail against the West for disturbing their peace, but they could scarcely regard themselves as pious Party members. Mr Mikoyan's face had been used as a dart-board to while away the long winter evenings.

'That is quite enough, Sergeant. You will confine yourselves to answering our questions, please.' Tania's voice broke sharply in, but Marcus scarcely heard her. He was thinking of what Goltz had said, and what he had seen as they drove into Rudisheim. A town of ten thousand inhabitants that had shrunk to less than three thousand since the war. Deserted streets, rows of empty houses and shops with boards nailed across the windows, bombed ruins that nobody had troubled to clear or rebuild, and piles of rubble spilling into the roads and pavements. A place where anything could be hidden. A place where the ground had been disturbed and the rats could multiply unchecked. A sickness of the soil, they had once considered plague: a contagion sent from the stars to trouble the earth and drive the animals up into the world of men. Goltz's claim that he knew all that went on in the town was obviously just an idle boast too. Neither he nor Braun would notice anything a yard away from their noses. Marcus had almost begun to despair of his hunch in coming to Rudisheim, but it had suddenly grown much stronger.

'Plague, Fräulein! Plague in Rudisheim!' A howl of derision from
the first pantomime lead brought him back to the present with a
jerk.

'No, Fräulein. We keep ourselves informed, you know. We read
the newspapers and listen to the radio, but, as I said before, it is just
propaganda. If there were any truth in this story of an epidemic
there would have been an outbreak in East Germany; cases here
in Rudisheim. Apart from a little influenza there is no illness in
this town. Ask anybody; the Mayor or Dr Humperdinck. Correct,
Comrade Braun?'

'Perfectly correct, Comrade Goltz. We are a healthy people in
these parts; perhaps the healthiest in Germany. It may be because
of the pine forests around us.' As though to prove the point Braun
inflated his chest till it appeared in danger of bursting. A huge grey
wolf crouched before the pig's flimsy home. 'I'll huff and I'll puff
and I'll blow your house down.'

'Yes, you look healthy enough, gentlemen, but I wonder how
long you will remain so. You obviously have no idea of the speed at
which this thing can travel, nor just how horrible its symptoms are.
No, as a doctor, I wouldn't gamble on your chances of remaining
healthy for very much longer.' Marcus had the satisfaction of seeing them wilt slightly before his professional stare.

'Now tell me something. Have either of you heard the story of
the Black Virgin?'

'The Black Virgin?' Braun frowned for a second and then burst
into a roar of laughter. 'No, that is a new one to me, Herr Doktor.
You tell it to us and I will tell you the one about the railway porter
who had three testicles.'

'Silence, constable. You should be ashamed of yourself, Comrade Braun.' Goltz scowled at him and nodded to Marcus.

'Yes, I know the story, Herr Doktor, but you have got it wrong.
It is not "virgin", but "woman" that she is called. A hag who rides
about the woods on the shoulders of a dead man. It is just a legend,
of course; a folk-tale like the Rhinegold or the dragons in the valley of the Neckar . . .'

'Or the head of Rudolph.' Braun broke in, quite unabashed by
his rebuff.

'You know about that?' Marcus frowned, remembering the account he had read in Vogel's *Great Pandemic*. 'The relic that was kept in the church?'

'But naturally, Herr Doktor. Before it was stolen everybody in Rudisheim knew about it. The head of a monk cast in bronze, I think. It was supposed to be Rudolph von Ginter, the mad abbot who died in the Middle Ages and was taken away by the Devil, but nobody was sure about that, of course. I have seen it, though, and such a face he had: like a damned soul who has been a long time in the fire.'

'There was a story about it, too.' Goltz interrupted him. If there was to be a lecture on local antiquities, his rank obviously entitled him to give it before a mere constable.

'The head was supposed to be hollow and there was something inside it; something very valuable. One day a man would discover the secret of how to open it and then . . .' He broke off, staring sheepishly at the floor. 'It was all nonsense, of course; just a fairy tale for children.'

'And it disappeared at the end of the war?'

'That is right, Herr Doktor. Some D.P.s from Reichburg camp are supposed to have stolen it. That was never proved, of course. All we know is that no local people would have dared to take the relic. At any rate, the church was bombed and it vanished. I was not here myself, but a prisoner of war in England.' He looked at Marcus as though he were personally responsible. 'In Yorkshire, near a place called Huddersfield. Do you know Huddersfield, Herr Doktor? It is not a very nice town, I think.'

'It is a horrible town. But tell me, Sergeant, is there anybody in Rudisheim who could give me a full account of the relic and the local legends? The priest perhaps? The schoolmaster, or this Dr Humperdinck?'

'No, there is no priest any more and the schoolmaster and the doctor have only been here a few years. There is a local history book in the library, but it won't tell you any more than I can. There's no more to tell really. Just a bronze head and a lot of silly legends about it.'

'What about Karl von Arnim, Comrade?'

'*Von* Arnim, Comrade Braun?' Goltz snorted with annoyance. 'This is a democratic country and we no longer use "von".'

'All the same, if you are interested in our legends, Herr Doktor, Karl Arnim is the man to help you. His father, the old Freiherr, was pastor here till after the war and he lives with his mother in the church house. He works as a sort of park-keeper; looking after the abbey grounds and so on. The family have been here for generations. I think it was his great-great-grandfather who built the church in the first place.'

'Thank you.' Marcus made a note of the name. 'But just now you told us that no local people would have dared to take the relic. Why is that, Sergeant? After all, you mentioned a treasure.'

'Yes, there was a treasure; a wonderful treasure; the most valuable thing in the world, they said. Just a silly story, of course.' Goltz shook his head, but there was a sudden gleam in his eye and all at once he looked more like an eager boy than an ogre. Marcus realized that at least one child had believed in fairy tales; had known that there was a crock of gold at the end of the rainbow; that the noises in the attic were not merely boards creaking; that there really was something walking through the dark woods at night.

'But if there was a treasure, why wasn't the relic removed years ago? Surely somebody would have stolen it before, or at least tried to open it? After all, it wasn't locked up. It just stood there in the church, didn't it? Quite an easy thing to steal, I should have thought.'

'Yes, it would have been easy, Herr Doktor. All the same, nobody would have laid a finger on that relic – nobody from Rudisheim. There was more to the story than just a treasure – that stupid story to frighten children.' Goltz looked down at the floor and it was clear that as a child he hadn't found the story at all stupid.

'You see, they told us that the head of Rudolph von Ginter had a guardian.'

Fifteen

'This is the radio service of the East German People's Republic. We are about to break off transmission for three minutes and will then bring you an announcement of the utmost national importance. Will you please inform your neighbours of this? I repeat that the announcement is of the utmost . . .'

Well, here it is – here it comes at last. Kirk stared through the window of the ante-room beside the operating theatre. The Linden outside was deserted and the snow lay thick and unmarked on the pavements. Not for long he thought. Soon the crowds would be coming out; pouring down the streets to hospitals and inoculation centres, just as they were doing in England. As he'd said, the wall couldn't hold it back and the thing was starting to spread across the world. He heard Petrov's coffee cup rattle as the radio came to life again.

'Plague . . . bubonic plague.' An announcer with a reassuring voice gave almost the same message as he himself had vetted in London. 'Plague . . . Three cases confirmed in East Berlin . . . Plague . . . No cause for alarm, and immunization centres are being set up at the following points . . . Plague . . . The authorities are confident that the outbreak will soon be under full control, and ample stocks of serum are available . . . Plague . . . Plague . . . bubonic plague . . .' Like a cracked gramophone record the sentences kept repeating themselves and Kirk closed his eyes for a moment. 'The authorities will soon have the outbreak under full control.' Lies that wouldn't fool anybody for long. They might slow the epidemic down while the stocks of serum lasted, but without knowing the source of the bacillus or having a drug which would kill it, the death-roll was bound to multiply every hour.

'Shall we go back?' Petrov switched off the set. Until a few minutes ago he had been working the Morse key for almost an hour and his wrist felt as though it were paralysed. 'I don't suppose there has been any reaction but . . .' He shrugged his shoulders and walked into the operating theatre. His assistant had taken over the key and the buzzer still creaked like a cicada across the room.

'Der der dot – dot dot dot dot – dot . . . Where did the boy come from, Gustav? Who brought him into West Berlin? Who is Gretel, Gustav? Who are Iron Hans and Clever Gretel . . .' He shook his head as he saw them return.

'He still doesn't respond then?' Petrov nodded and looked at Kirk. 'Well, our gamble doesn't seem to have paid off, I'm afraid. Any other ideas?'

'No, not at the moment.' Kirk studied the still figure on the table. Behr's eyes were fixed on the ceiling, and he appeared to be smiling at it. His body was quite motionless and his hand on the key looked as dead as that of a wax dummy.

'No, I've no more ideas for the present. Let's just hope that the lab. boys come up with something soon. Let's hope that Marcus Levin's hunch was not as crazy as it sounded.'

'It is no use, gentlemen. No use at all.' Another doctor had joined the first and he ran a lens over Behr's eyes and shook his head. 'The Psilocybin has taken all right. This man wants to communicate, but he just hasn't got the strength to do so. I don't know how long he will live, but I think your best chance is to let him rest for a few minutes. I'll increase the oxygen and perhaps . . .' He shrugged his shoulders and started to adjust a tap on one of the cylinders.

'As you say, Doctor. You can stop sending for a moment.' Petrov motioned to the operator. Though the room was warm he pulled his jacket a little tighter around him.

'Didn't you hear me? I told you to stop.' The buzzer was still working, though the Morse sounded slower and more indistinct. 'Are you blind as well as . . . ?' He broke off as he looked at his assistant. The man was busily writing on a pad and it was the other key that was activating the buzzer. Slow and faltering, but gathering speed at every impulse, Gustav Behr's finger had begun to tap out a message.

★　★　★

The snow had stopped at last and in the thin moonlight the streets of Rudisheim looked as though the war had only recently ended. At least a third of the buildings were bombed ruins; little or no attempt had been made to clear away the rubble. Even the coal-mine that had given the place its pre-war importance was a ruin, with the lift headgear standing out like a blighted tree in the car headlights.

'Just what do you expect to learn from this man, Mark?' Tania frowned as he negotiated a bend. Since reaching Rudisheim they had reached first-name terms and she had finally allowed him to drive.

'I'm not sure. About the local fairy tales perhaps. In which part of the forest the Plague Maiden rides her corpse. What was the thing that was supposed to guard the relic and failed so miserably.'

'You're not serious, Mark? You don't really believe that there can be any connection between those old stories and the epidemic?' She twisted round on the seat, staring at him and laying her hand on his arm. 'You're joking, aren't you?'

'No, I'm not joking at all. Until I've talked to this local antiquary, Arnim, I'm perfectly serious.' Through his coat Marcus seemed to feel the warmth of Tania's fingers.

'I also want to know about the people who live round here. Is there a family, on a farm perhaps or in some remote house, who, for no reason, have been shunned and disliked by their neighbours for generations? A very intermarried family, probably, because few outsiders would marry into it.'

'For no reason? That's ridiculous, Mark! There's always a reason for everything.'

'Quite right. I mean for no apparent reason. If these people exist, nobody knows why they must be shunned except that it is thought unsafe to associate with them.'

'Just a moment: I think I'm beginning to understand what you mean.' Tania's frown deepened. 'These spores you described can exist almost indefinitely, in the soil perhaps. You are suggesting that people living near them might have been infected, but somehow grown . . . ?' She struggled for the right word.

'Might have developed immunity.' Marcus nodded. 'Yes, that's partly it. Strange cases of immunity exist, you know. The typhoid carrier is unaffected by the disease, but his faeces pass it on to others. The rat flea, *Xenopsylla cheopis*, carries the plague bacillus but suffers no ill effects from it.

'What I'm driving at is something called "regenerative mutation": a change in the actual bacillus itself. The organism enters the blood stream of an immune host and at once becomes dormant. For thousands of generations it remains static and the host is quite unaware of its presence and also incapable of passing the disease on. But from time to time and for short periods only, you get a generation which is active. During those periods, the host will be a carrier.'

'And you think that Billy Fenwick might have been in contact with such a carrier? A perfectly innocent person who thought there was nothing wrong with him?'

'I don't think anything, my dear. I'm just clutching at all the straws that come my way.' There you go admitting it, he thought. Sir Marcus Levin, the specialist, the expert, the bringer of hope and confidence, following a blind hunch and clutching at straws because there was nothing else to clutch at. 'All the same, the fact that there was no early outbreak in East Germany makes it a possibility at least . . . This must be it, I think.'

He stopped the car and climbed out, feeling slightly better for the cold air on his face. To their right was a small wood and behind it a ruined church. There had once been a track for vehicles, but a rusty chain was drawn across it and the only entrance was through a wicket gate. He pulled it back for Tania and they walked down the path. Beneath the thick covering of snow there were deep ruts and furrows, and among the trees brambles had been allowed to grow unchecked, almost blocking the way. Karl Arnim didn't appear to take his park-keeping duties very seriously. Probably, like Goltz and Braun, he had suffered no outside inspection for years.

'Brrr! What do you say in English? Yes, it gives me the creeps.' Tania's hand tightened on his arm as the wood ended and a graveyard opened up before them: marble crosses and broken pillars and weeping nymphs bearing urns.

'You can say that again.' Marcus nodded, but these graves didn't

interest him. Their tombstones were all modern or late nine-
teenth century. The dead he feared had been buried for six hundred
years. Behind them the church stood out like a great stone ship
and, though half the roof had fallen in, it looked enormous in the
moonlight with a huge square tower and flying buttresses straining
against the walls.

'Listen, though.' In the far distance there was a sharp humming
sound coming towards them and growing louder at every second.
As it approached the earth shook slightly, the noise increased to
the choking roar of a diesel engine and then started to fade away.
There must be a deep cutting somewhere behind the church because there was no sight of the train.

A cutting. Billy Fenwick had said that when he came round he
was lying in a deep cutting and a woman was bending over him.
As far as the route was concerned they could be in the right place.
Marcus walked on through the graveyard. Though Karl Arnim
might not be a competent park-keeper, he obviously kept his own
house in good repair. It stood a little to the left of the church, with
its windows brightly lit and smoke eddying from the tall chimneys.
Under the snow-covered roof it looked strangely unreal: a ginger-
bread house tucked away in the forest to lure unwary travellers to
their doom.

There had been a lot of fairy stories lately, Marcus thought.
A lot of Grimm; Iron Hans, Clever Gretel, Brother Lustig – and
now this. As he raised the brass knocker, he half expected to hear
a window creak open and a crone's voice intone, 'Nibble, nibble,
mousekin. Who's nibbling at my housekin?'

'Come in please, sir, and you too, Fräulein. Come in at once. It is
a terrible night.' Frau Arnim smiled at them as she pulled back the
door. Though she was certainly old, nobody could have described
her as a crone, for she was short and stout and looked as brisk as
a terrier, with white hair tied back in a bun and little bulging eyes
beaming in welcome.

'Ah, that's better, isn't it?' She slammed the door to as though
shutting out an unwanted visitor. 'Now, let's put down your coats
over here.' As she fussed around them Marcus had the feeling that
they were two delicate children in charge of a nanny.

'My son would have gone down to the road to meet you, but they only telephoned us a minute ago.'

'You knew we were coming then?' Marcus glanced around the little hall-cum-sitting room. The walls were bright with polished brass and flower prints and Dresden china figures. The general effect was of over-cosiness.

'Yes, of course. Fasholt and Fafner telephoned us. Oh, I'm sorry.' She shook her head and laughed. 'We call our policemen, Goltz and Braun, that; after the giants in the Rhinegold, of course.' She radiated cheery goodwill and must have been a model parson's wife; an organizer of sales of work, a visitor of the poor, an encourager of the sick.

'But what is my son up to? Surely he must have heard us.' She bustled to the foot of the stairs and raised her voice. 'Karl, Karl, our guests are here.'

'I am just coming, Mutti. I thought I should put on another suit in their honour.' Karl Arnim must have been at least fifty years old, but his face was quite unlined as though the years had written nothing on it. Apart from a white collar he was dressed in black and, if Goltz had not told him otherwise, Marcus would have taken him for a clergyman.

'Fräulein.' He gave Tania a little awkward bow and held out his hand to Marcus. 'I know of you by reputation, sir,' he said. 'It is a very great privilege to welcome you under our roof. But please come through into my study.' His eyes twinkled as he pulled open a door. 'My mother is very proud of her brass and china; but they make the place rather bright for me. A real palace, isn't it, Sir Marcus? Circe's palace, perhaps.'

'It is very nice indeed.' Marcus felt slightly embarrassed as he smiled back. A real palace to describe a bright little hall. Circe's palace, the place where men were turned into swine.

'Now do sit down, both of you. Over there would be best, I think.' Arnim motioned them towards a big porcelain stove. 'It is still bitterly cold.'

'Thank you.' Marcus stared around the room as he sat down. 'Den' was the obvious word to describe it; like Arnim's clothes, it savoured of the clerical. Old leather armchairs, leather-bound

books in tall oak cases, photographs of student groups and an illuminated testimonial that read 'Presented to Freiherr Walther von
Arnim by his devoted parishioners.'

'Did the – the giants tell you what I wanted to see you about,
Herr Arnim?'

'Fasholt attempted to.' Arnim sat down very close to his mother
and Marcus sensed that if they were alone their hands would be
touching. 'Goltz and Braun really are like giants, aren't they? Great,
stupid, clumsy giants, but we are fortunate in having them when
one considers the majority of the Vopo.

'Yes, Goltz said that you would like to consult me about our
local folk-lore. Though I am no trained historian, I will be delighted
to tell you all I do know.'

'Thank you.' Marcus studied Arnim, remembering what the
police had said about him. The Arnim family had lived in Rudisheim for generations and Karl had been on the point of taking
holy orders when the war had come and he had been carried off to
the army. He had been wounded in Africa and shipped home like
a piece of useless rubbish. By the time he recovered the war was
over, the Russians had occupied that part of Germany and there
was no church for him to serve. A bitter, frustrated man, one would
have thought, but there was nothing except rather foolish good
humour in his face.

'Don't thank me, Sir Marcus,' he said. 'I am most flattered by
your visit. Just as I was impressed when I read your paper on the
"Streptothra Madura Fungus" some time ago.'

'You have studied medicine then?'

'Studied it, but never qualified.' Arnim shook his head. 'I always
wanted to be a medical missionary, but fate was against it. Nowadays you could describe me as an amateur in everything, I'm afraid.
An amateur botanist, an amateur historian, even an amateur park-
keeper. There is no doubt that I hold my job more as a sinecure
than anything else.'

'Karl would have been a great doctor, Sir Marcus.' As though
she couldn't resist touching him, Frau Arnim's right hand gripped
her son's. Her index finger was rather unpleasantly deformed: it
had no joint, and the nail grew where the knuckle should have

been. 'He was admitted to Heidelberg when he was only seventeen and Professor Mainz described him as one of the most brilliant students he had ever known.'

'Please, Mutti, you are embarrassing me.' Arnim withdrew his hand and reached out towards a pile of papers on the table.

'At any rate, let us hope that my small gifts as an amateur local historian may be of some use to you, Sir Marcus.' He picked up a photograph and handed it across to him. 'Sergeant Goltz mentioned a few of the things you wanted to hear about. This was one of them, I think.'

'Yes, that is one of them.' The picture was almost life-size, and it showed the face of a man fashioned from some coarse metal. The features were so bloated as to appear scarcely human and the description 'lion-faced' came automatically to Marcus as he looked at it. Though taken after death the expression showed not only pain and terror, but also murderous rage, and he remembered Goltz's description of the relic. 'Such a face he had; like a damned soul who has been a long time in the fire.'

'Yes, that's the death mask of the mad abbot, Sir Marcus. What do you want to know about it?'

'Almost everything that you can tell me.' Marcus considered how to explain. 'Did you hear the news flash on the radio just now?'

'A news flash?' Arnim frowned and shook his head. 'No, we don't listen to the radio very often these days . . . But, Mutti, I am sure that our guests are very cold and would like a cup of coffee.'

He smiled as she got up and hurried to the door, and then stopped smiling. His unlined face suddenly looked much older and there was strain and unhappiness in the eyes.

'Sir Marcus,' he said, as the door closed behind her. 'Please forgive me. I lied to you just now. I did hear the bulletin, but I don't want my mother to know about the outbreak; not for the time being, at least. She has an almost pathological terror of disease, and I'd like to keep it from her till the morning. My father died of cancer, you see. He died very horribly and he took a long time over it. Since then, every room in the house, except this one, has been dusted and polished at least once a day.' Arnim leaned forward and opened the damper of the stove.

'Yes, I heard about the epidemic, Sir Marcus, and I guessed that that might be your reason for coming to Rudisheim.'

'You guessed that, did you? Why, Herr Arnim? Have you some evidence that it might originate from around here?'

'No, no evidence, but surely there must be a connection? An outbreak of *bacillus pestis* in East Germany and a distinguished bacteriologist coming to Rudisheim and asking questions about a man who died of plague in the fourteenth century. Can you tell me why you have come, Sir Marcus?'

'I'll tell you all I can.' As Marcus spoke he realized that there was something in Arnim's make-up that made him an ideal listener: the aura of a priest in the confessional, the manner of a psychiatrist quietly taking notes beside the couch. He told him all he knew and also what he merely suspected; his vague theory about a return to the Black Death bacillus and regenerative mutations.

'Thank you. You have been most kind to confide in me.' Arnim got up and pulled an old, battered volume from the nearest bookcase. 'But tell me something else, Sir Marcus. Do you believe in evil, and the punishment of evil?'

'Evil? I believe in wickedness as part of the human predicament; a necessary piece of the process of evolution.'

'Yes, as a good scientist, I thought you would say that. Human wickedness; as men progress from apes to the Übermensch perhaps.' Arnim smiled as he flicked through the pages. 'I don't mean that I'm afraid. I mean pure evil which comes from outside; from the devil, for lack of a better word.' He had found his place at last and held the book under the light.

'This is a fairly early account of the head of von Ginter. Please excuse my reading it to you. The print is rather bad and it is in medieval dog Latin.

' "And when Lucifer had taken the soul of Rudolph, our abbot, and all men knew what his life had been, we made a bronze image of his face which will stand in the porch of our church. And in the image we have locked a demon that will watch over this accursed place for ever."

'Yes, we are a superstitious people around here, Sir Marcus. Children still claim to see the Plague Woman riding her corpse. Grown men avoid certain parts of the woods at night because of the wolf-rat on whom it is death to look.' Arnim still smiled, but Marcus could see that, like the policemen, he had once believed the stories implicitly.

'And do you think those legends are all nonsense, Sir Marcus? Don't you think it is possible that there might have been a demon or guardian in that relic?'

'If there were, it wasn't very effective, Herr Arnim. After all, the relic was stolen by D.P.s at the end of the war.'

'It was said to have been stolen. A great many people went to a lot of trouble to blame those D.P.s for it. Does the name Maria Trude mean anything to you?'

'Trude? You mean Frau Trude?' Marcus nodded. Another fairy-tale character to join Iron Hans and Clever Gretel and Brother Lustig. 'The woman who turned a curious girl into a log of wood and threw her on the fire?'

'Oh, no, not the witch out of Grimm. Maria Trude, or Frau Doktor Trude, was a very real person. With your background you must have heard of her, Sir Marcus. After all she was Julius Streicher's cousin. She was also in charge of the S.S. medical research centre at Dachau for a time.'

'Yes, I remember.' Twenty years slipped away for a moment and terror and hatred were like a red screen in front of Marcus's eyes, blinding him. 'She was supposed to have been killed in Berlin, but they never found the body. Why do you mention her now, Herr Arnim? What connection was there between Maria Trude and this?' He looked at the bronze face glowering across at him from the table.

'Because she may have had the relic, Sir Marcus. It was almost the last week of the war and everything was in chaos. We wanted to go to the west before the Russians arrived, but my father was dying and couldn't be moved. One evening that woman came here with a party of S.S. They said they were looking for an escaped prisoner and searched the church. Soon after they left, there was an air raid and the church was bombed. In the morning the relic was missing. It may have been buried under rubble and later found by D.P.s. There may have been an escaped prisoner, but personally I doubt it. You have known those people, Sir Marcus. Doesn't it seem feasible to you that Maria Trude might have wanted that relic?'

'But why, what possible motive could she have had?' Though Marcus muttered the question aloud, he knew the answer. Germany was breaking up and the sane thing would have been to find a disguise and a new personality before the Allied armies took over. Those people hadn't been sane, though. Himmler had sat in Flensburg consulting the Norse runes. Goering had imagined himself to be an honoured guest of the Americans. Hitler had bent over a map and moved armies which no longer existed. It was quite possible that Maria Trude could have based her security on a folk-tale.

'Yes, just a fairy tale, Sir Marcus.' Karl Arnim had exactly read his thoughts and he nodded across the firelight. 'Just a silly tale for children, but don't you think a woman like Maria Trude might have believed it?'

'She might have. All the same there was pretty clear evidence that she was killed in Berlin . . . Are you all right?'

Marcus broke off abruptly, because Arnim was obviously not listening. He was staring at the door with his lips drawn back and his face didn't look completely sane. 'Are you ill?'

'What's that? No, I'm all right, but listen for a moment. For God's sake keep quiet.' As he spoke the sound of a radio announcement grew in volume and flooded through the door. 'We repeat that there is no cause for alarm and ample stocks of serum are available . . .'

'Mutti. She turned on the wireless.' Arnim lurched across the room like a man in the last stages of Parkinson's disease. 'I meant to take out a valve, but with your coming there was no time; there was no time for anything.'

He pulled open the door and the announcer's voice poured unchecked into the room. 'Immunization centres are being set up at the following points . . .' At the same instant Marcus was on his feet and hurrying after him. Frau Arnim was standing in the centre of the hall swaying from side to side. Her eyes were wide open, as though staring at something which terrified her, and there was a line of foam around her mouth.

Sixteen

Trude – Maria Trude. As Marcus hurried down the path, the name seemed to beat in time to his footsteps. Was Karl Arnim's story even remotely possible, he wondered, or was the man so obsessed with the lost relic and his ideas of impersonal evil that a vague suspicion had grown into belief? Certainly there was a good deal of mental disturbance in his background. Though he was not a nerve specialist, Marcus had had little difficulty in diagnosing epilepsy as Frau Arnim had pitched forward with the radio blaring around her.

At any rate, true or false, he had to get the information to Kirk and Petrov. The Arnims' phone was out of order, probably the line had been brought down by snow. He only hoped it was a local fault and he could get through from Rudisheim.

'Mark, please listen to me. What I want to tell you is important.' He could feel Tania tugging at his sleeve, but he shrugged her aside and hurried on. He had to concentrate – to remember what he knew about the Trude woman. She had been a bacteriologist, that was certain. Worked on vegetable pathology as well. Oswald Farquhar had mentioned one of her papers in his Presidential Address last year. Yes, something about tobacco blight, 'Über die Mosaikkrankheit der Tabakspflanze.' Farquhar had used it as an example of how a really brilliant mind could sometimes fasten on to a wrong premise and fly completely off at a tangent.

But was it possible that she could be alive? At the time it had appeared quite certain that she had been killed in Berlin. Though they had never recovered the body, there had been enough witnesses to make it appear definite. There had been a thorough investigation too. Once it was discovered what had been happening at that research establishment – experiments into the causes of malignancy with paraffin and radiation cancers produced on human subjects – she'd been quite high up on the list of wanted war criminals.

But if she wasn't dead? If somehow her death had been faked then he could believe Arnim's story all right. If Trude's mind had

ran along the same lines as his own and she had suspected what
that relic might contain . . .

Marcus shuddered slightly at the thought. A crazy woman hiding under another name for twenty years. Quite an old woman, but
still bitter, still carrying on her crusade against the world. He was
quite sure now that he knew what the guardian of the relic was,
and he could picture her opening the case, studying the thing inside, gloating at the thought of its power, building up her phantasies of destruction. Then, one day, the phantasies had become too
strong to be resisted any more and the demon had been released
from its bottle to plague the earth.

'In a minute, my dear. Tell me in a minute, but please let me try
to concentrate a bit longer.' He climbed into the car as Tania broke
in again. Kirk had been sceptical enough about his going to Rudisheim and probably this new development would be received with
a good deal of disbelief. All the same it was at least something to go
on, and it would be a near miracle if they got anything out of Behr.

'But what on earth! Just what are you doing?' He swung round
as Tania reached out and snatched the car keys out of his hand.
'Look, I told you we have to get through to Berlin at once.'

'Yes, so you have told me, Mark.' She laid the keys out of his
reach on her side of the seat.

'You have also told me a lot of your theories, but now you are
going to hear one of mine.' As though there was not the slightest
need to hurry she pulled a packet of cigarettes out of her bag.

'Sir Marcus Levin, K.C.B., whatever that may mean,' she said
when at last the cigarette was alight. 'Mark Levin, the great bacteriologist who forgets all his scientific training and rushes blindly
off after every shred of evidence that comes his way. No, don't interrupt me.' She held the keys up to the window. 'Just sit still or I'll
throw them out into the snow.

'Now, Mark, you were quite right in coming to Rudisheim and
in a moment I'll prove it to you. But this story about the Nazi doctor that Arnim told you! You can't believe that. Arnim is trying to
hide something and he made it up on the spur of the moment. All
that business about the S.S. coming here! Oh, I realize that with
your background everything about the Nazis must seem like a per-

sonal war, but the Trude woman is dead. She was killed when our troops entered Berlin.'

'Tania, you said that you can prove I was right in coming here. Have you got some evidence? Something I don't know about?'

'Yes, I think I have, Mark, and in a minute I'll tell you what it is, but first I want to ask you a question. When you examined the Fenwick boy, did you notice if he had buck teeth?'

'Buck teeth?' Marcus frowned. He could almost see the rash on Billy's chest again and feel the bubo throbbing under his fingers, but the face . . . ? Apart from the fact that it had been flushed and bloated he could hardly recall what it had looked like.

'I can't really remember,' he said. 'I can't be sure, but I seem to think that he may have had. But why do you want to know? What possible importance can it have?'

'It may have every importance, Mark. It may tell us exactly what happened to him.' Tania fumbled in her handbag and brought out something which glittered under the dashboard light. 'When Arnim's mother had that attack he told me there was a bottle of tablets in the bathroom cupboard and I got them for her.'

'Yes, I remember, but so what? They were only pheno-barbitone. A perfectly normal prescription for cases like that. She was much better as soon as she took one.'

'She was better, but that's not the important thing. You see, beside those tablets, I found this.' She handed him the small and rather unpleasant object, smiling at his expression as he looked at it.

'Yes, it's strange, isn't it, Mark? You said that you seem to remember that the boy may have had buck teeth. Doesn't it start to fit together at last? After all, what possible use could an old woman or a middle-aged man have for a child's dental brace?'

*　　*　　*

'Dot – der der dot – der der der . . .' Behr's fingers still trembled on the Morse key, but the impulses were very slow now and more often than not they were just a jumble of sound without any meaning at all.

'Dot dot dot – der der derrrrrr . . .' They finally stopped altogether and his finger came to rest pressing down the connection. The doctor felt briefly for the pulse and shook his head.

'Well, that's it, comrade. He's dead and in my mind it's a wonder that he lasted so long. I hope you've got what you want.'

'Give it to me.' Petrov had been staring over his assistant's shoulder and he snatched the pad from him, studying the disjointed sentences, and the letters which often didn't add up to a word, and here and there blank spaces where the dots and dashes hadn't signified a letter. For a full ten minutes he pored over the pages, his pencil crossing out and adding and joining up as he struggled to make the meaning clear and then his face broke into a grin of delight and he turned to Kirk.

'Well, General, we've done it, I think. This is all we wanted to know and I'd like to congratulate you on a most brilliant idea.' Petrov waved the pad in his hand and he almost capered in triumph.

'Yes, it's all here. The child fell from the train and was befriended by what you would call the "Resistance Movement" and I the "Counter-revolutionary Element". The person who found him was this Clever Gretel of whom we have heard so much. He was later smuggled into West Berlin by what Behr refers to as the "Meister-Route".

'Get my car round to the door, please.' He nodded to his assistant and scowled at the still body on the table. The doctor had already pulled a sheet over its face.

'And I thought that that piece of carrion was my friend, but he knew everything, and rather than betray his precious organization he was prepared to gamble with the health of the world.'

'Yes, I suppose he was.' Though every news flash reported that the epidemic was gathering strength, Kirk still felt sympathy for Gustav Behr. 'But did he tell us who this Gretel is and where we can find him?'

'Yes, he told us everything, but it's a she, not a he, as we thought. Her name really is Gretel, and she's been very clever indeed. Let's go and pay a call on her.' He clapped Kirk on the shoulder and moved towards the door still squinting at the pad.

'And we've done Marcus Levin a grave injustice, I'm afraid. We both thought he had rushed off on a fool's errand and we were quite wrong.

'The woman we want lives at Rudisheim, and her name is Gretel Arnim.'

Seventeen

'Any luck? Did you get through to Berlin?' Marcus started the engine as Tania hurried back from the telephone booth.

'I got through, but it was no use. Petrov and Kirk left the hospital, but didn't go back to police headquarters. I gave a message for them.'

'Very well.' Marcus glanced at his watch and drove off. Almost nine thirty already; over twenty minutes since Tania had shown him the dental brace. She had been in favour of knocking up Goltz and Braun and taking them round to Arnim's house, but he had quashed that. The men had not been inoculated and, if Billy Fenwick really had been with the Arnims, it would be murder to take them there. He had made her try to contact Kirk and Petrov and now it was up to him.

Not that there was any definite evidence yet. The brace might have belonged to any child; a nephew or niece of the Arnims, perhaps, who had stayed with them and left it behind. He couldn't even be certain that Billy Fenwick had had protruding teeth.

All the same ... Marcus remembered the hint of mania in Arnim's face as he discussed the relic and how his mother had stood swaying in the hall with foam on her lips and the radio blaring around her. He stopped the car at the end of the drive and slipped the brace into his pocket.

'All right, here goes. Let's find out for ourselves.' He opened the door and climbed out.

It was much darker now. A wind had blown in from the north, bringing thin trails of cloud to obscure the moon. Their feet slipped and stumbled on the frozen path, and among the trees briars clutched at them like small, vicious hands. There was a haze of mist drifting across the tombstones which made them resemble

yew hedges, trained and clipped for centuries in an English park, or
the strange fungoid vegetation of some distant planet.

But what was he going to say to them? What the hell was he
going to say to the Arnims? A dozen scenes from stage and cinema
crossed Marcus's mind. The great detective smiling cynically as the
malefactor made his glib denials. The flick of a finger, the lost heir-
ess coming in from the wings, and the damning evidence trium-
phantly produced. 'And how exactly do you explain this?'

'Mark, are you sure that we're doing the right thing? Don't you
think we should wait till we can contact Petrov? After all, if these
people really are what we think . . . ?' Tania's fingers gripped his
hand, making him think of warm things: log fires and double beds
and a final drink before turning in.

'No, I'm not sure about anything, my dear,' he said. 'And, if you
prefer it, give me that revolver I saw in your handbag and go back
to the car. I'm not waiting any longer to contact Kirk and Petrov.
I've got to know the truth now.

'Make up your mind, please.' He watched her hesitate and then
fall into step beside him, and he knew he was right. There was no
time to wait for reinforcements. That child's dental brace was the
only real clue they had and he had to check it.

All the same, he half hoped that it meant nothing; that the
Arnims were just unbalanced eccentrics with a perfectly normal explanation for the brace. And if the Arnims were innocent, he even
hoped that the story about Maria Trude was rubbish too. He hoped
that there was no human agency involved and all he had to deal
with was a freak of nature.

As before, the little house still looked bright and cheerful, with
lights glowing through the curtains and the chimney smoke plum-
ing in the wind. Once again he lifted the little brass knocker, trying
to imagine how he would conduct the interview. As he brought it
down the door swung back a few inches as though the catch were
free but a chain was holding it.

'Herr Arnim,' he called. 'Are you there, Herr Arnim?' He
knocked again, feeling the door move another inch and he knew
that it wasn't a chain, but something soft and heavy which was behind it.

'Mark, look! Look down at your feet, Mark!' Tania's breath was like smoke in the freezing air and, as he followed her eyes, Marcus stiffened. The cottage floor sloped slightly and in the light from the room he could see a trickle of dark liquid dripping over the door-step and reddening the snow that was piled against it. He hurled his shoulder against the door and forced back the thing which was holding it.

'Let me die.' Frau Arnim lay on her side staring up at him and she looked like a tired child wanting to go to bed. 'Please, please let me die.' She still held the knife in her right hand, but her left couldn't have held anything. She had slashed the muscles as well as the artery and he could see a glint of white bone through the ooz-ing blood.

'Yes, yes, you will sleep soon.' Marcus pulled out his handker-chief and twisted it round her wrist with the door key to form a tourniquet, motioning to Tania as he did so. 'Try and find some-thing for her to drink; schnapps or brandy or anything at all.

'That should do.' He took the bottle of kümmel from her and forced it between the woman's lips. Most of it slopped on to the floor as she fought against him, but at least a little went down.

'Are you feeing better, Frau Arnim?' he said. 'Can you tell me what happened? Where your son is?'

'My son? I have no son, Herr Doktor.' Her lips were like grey worms crawling across her face. 'I killed my son years ago and he became something else. I destroyed him. Didn't you hear what he said, Herr Doktor? Circe's palace; the place where men are turned into swine.'

'Yes, I remember Frau Arnim.' Marcus picked her up and laid her on a sofa by the fire. 'But what happened after we left here? Why did you try to kill yourself?'

'Because I guessed what had happened after I heard the radio and I made Karl tell me everything . . . no, that will be no good to you.' She shook her head as Tania took a revolver from her bag and moved towards the study door.

'Karl has gone. He went away as soon as he told me what had happened . . .' Her voice was so weak that Marcus could hardly make out the words. '. . . to the little English boy.'

'Billy Fenwick?' He leaned forward till his ear was almost touching her mouth. 'He was here, then?'

'Yes, he was here. We found him lying by the railway line and brought him home. Poor little boy, he was so cold and frightened. When he told me who he was and what had happened I made arrangements with my friends to have him taken back to his own people.

'Karl didn't mind my bringing the boy here at first and then something made him angry. I think Billy laughed at him, but I never knew what it was about. I never imagined he would actually harm him though.

'And now please let me die, Herr Doktor. Can't you see that I have to die? I turned Karl into a monster and now . . .' She stared longingly at the knife on the floor. 'I often wondered what he was doing in the crypt, but I never guessed that he would hurt anybody. Please let me die.'

'You will sleep in a moment, Frau Arnim. I will help you to sleep, but you must help us first. Where did Karl go after he left you?'

'I don't know. He didn't tell me, but I think he would go to Berlin. He mentioned something about the new tunnel that our friends have made.'

'To Berlin.' Marcus looked up, but Tania had already hurried to the telephone at the top of the stairs and was rattling the rest up and down in the hope of getting a connection.

'And what did Karl do in the crypt, Frau Arnim?'

'He played, Herr Doktor. He always wanted to be a priest and he played at being one. He wanted power and esteem and the assurance that he wasn't just the pig I made him. Then one day he told me that he found – he found . . .' The eyes closed and her face went quite slack.

'Yes, I know what he found, Frau Arnim. The thing which could give him all the power he craved for.' Marcus suddenly remembered an illustration from a book of Greek legends: the inquisitive woman bent over a casket as she searched for the catch. Pandora's box opening and all the ills of heaven rushing out to plague mankind.

'The line is still down?' He nodded as Tania came back into the room.

'Yes, Frau Arnim should be all right. She's just passed out from loss of blood and nervous exhaustion. Try and tear a strip from that table-cloth, will you? I can't leave her with the tourniquet on. Good.' He bandaged the woman's arm tightly, removed the handkerchief and stood up.

'And now, let's go and see exactly what Karl did find in that crypt.' He shook his head at Tania's revolver. 'Yes, by all means take that if it makes you feel better, but I don't think it will be much use. The person we're going to meet died a long time ago.'

*　　*　　*

The church itself was just a ruin, of course. Even though the moon was partly hidden by cloud they could see that. The doors had rotted away from their hinges and lay on the floor covered by rubble, and most of the roof had fallen in. Through a gaping hole in the wall the clock hung face down over the nave with its hands set at twenty to three, and bushes and creepers had pushed up through the tiles of the chancel to screen the altar. It didn't look as though anybody had been near the place for years.

But that was wrong. Mingled with the smell of rubble and damp wood they could make out a tang of burning oil and hot metal. Tania's torch flitted across the building and she walked forward. To the right of the chancel a flight of stairs ran down to the crypt, and in the torch-light they could see that it had recently been swept. There was a rusty iron door at the foot of the stairs, but the key was on the outside and it swung open on well-oiled hinges.

'Yes, the blighter really did play at being a priest.' Marcus stared around the room. It was about forty feet long and almost the same width, with a vaulted ceiling and oil lamps burning along the walls. The general effect was a mixture of library and private chapel, for there were two long bookcases by the door and a curtain on the far wall with a rough wooden altar in front of it.

'A priest, and a scientist too.' He glanced at the books. Hirt's *Conquest of Plague*, Kuhn's *Vegetable Pathology*, Wilhelm Sahm's *History of the Plague in East Prussia*, his own monograph on the Madura fungus. From a hook at the side of the second case a cassock was hanging and he felt a sudden pity for Karl Arnim as he looked at it. A man obsessed with guilt and the sense of failure who had hidden something. A man full of hatred and bitterness which must have come to boiling point in that little cosy house by the grave-yard. And, one day, when he was cleaning the thing he had hidden, or merely examining its workmanship, he had discovered the secret and Pandora's box had clicked open.

Yes, Marcus felt that he knew everything now, and he walked very slowly towards the altar and the heap of faded purple cloth that lay on it. His heart was racing as he stretched out his hand and pulled at the cloth. It came away, falling in folds to the floor, some-thing glittered and he looked at the face of Rudolph von Ginter.

The chronicles had been incorrect, though. The thing was brass, not bronze, and time and weather must have given it the rough corroded appearance he had seen in the photograph. Now it had been cleaned and polished and shone like gold in the lamplight. Though cast after death there was no mistaking the agony of the expression, and 'lion-faced' was clear in every swollen feature.

'But how does it open? How did Arnim find what the demon really was?' Marcus took Tania's torch and craned forward over the relic. On the backward sweep of the skull, where the tonsure joined the carved hair, he found what he was looking for: a blur as though an artist's hand had shaken on his chisel; a line of scratches which might mean anything or nothing. He pulled out his lens and bent still lower. The scratches steadied themselves and became words; four lines of verse engraved with a needle on the shining metal.

Very carefully Marcus copied each letter on to his notebook and then looked at the result. At first they didn't appear to mean any-thing at all; just a jumble of words written in some language he couldn't recognize, though it had a Spanish flavour.

> Fincá los Inogos
> Que yacé alli l'Arca
> Do tusé una Marca
> Sobré los tus Ojos.

Yes, of course. He nodded as understanding came. The verse

didn't mean anything to him because it was written in a dead language. The words were Cid, twelfth-century medieval Spanish. And that was strange, because the relic itself was fourteenth century. They would have been as incomprehensible to a German of the period as to a present-day Englishman. The message must have been written that way so that it could be read only by a highly educated person.

Well, it was going to be read by a highly educated person. It was going to be read by Sir Marcus Levin, whose knowledge of medieval Spanish might be scanty, but whose linguistic ability was certainly not. He bent over the notebook, concentrating hard and jotting down every word he could recognize from its modern form.

'Marca' – that was obvious. 'Inogos' was knees, and 'Ojos' – eyes; while 'Arca' was a chest – perhaps a treasure chest. His hand ran across the page and soon he had what he imagined to be a rough translation.

> Bend your knees
> The treasure lies
> Where I cut a mark
> Above your eyes.

'Bend your knees'? Why so? Couldn't he see every detail of the thing much better by holding it to the light? No, of course he couldn't. The point was that the light had to be above the eyes and he remembered the purpose for which the relic had been designed. It was to stand in the porch of a church and before it the faithful would kneel in terror. Probably its makers had intended anybody who could actually read the message to see what it contained, but the religious community had died, the monastery had fallen into ruin, and oxidation had hidden the words till Karl Arnim's polishing operations revealed them.

Very well, he would bend his knees, if that was what was wanted. Marcus lowered himself before the altar, and he could see at last. In that position the light was reflected from the polished chin to the curve of the swollen, arrogant lip and showed the thing which lay below it; a tiny hairline crack into which a fingernail could just be inserted. He reached for the crack and very gently pressed upwards. The front of the relic tilted back like a visor and the demon of Rudisheim stared out at him.

'Yes, there it is. There's your guardian. There's the Gorgon that can turn you to stone.' Sweat was pouring down his forehead, but Marcus felt no horror, nor even disgust. The thing was too sad, too pathetic for that. The dreadful leather thing, wedged in its case, with two huge rubies which were its treasure gleaming in the eye sockets, and blackened teeth grinning between the ridges that had once been lips. The face of a man who had died six hundred years ago and looked like a tortured monkey, buried alive in the shining brass.

'But how did he discover that the stuff was still active?'

Marcus spoke to himself, and then swung round as he heard Tania scream. He had just time to see Karl Arnim rushing towards him, and then something swung out, picked him up, and threw him into oblivion.

Eighteen

He was lying in bright sunlight and it was very painful to his eyes. He was cold, too; lying somewhere high up on the white wall of a mountain, and the summit was only a few hundred feet above him. Soon he would get to his feet and climb up to that summit, but not for a moment. For a few more minutes he had to lie still and wait for the pain to stop.

'Mark, come round. Please come round, my dear.' The snow was pillowed under his head and somebody was speaking to him in Russian, which was ridiculous. What was he doing on a mountain, when he should be addressing the Royal Society on the enterin virus? Why was he so cold, and what was the thing that was beating on his head like a hammer?

'Please open your eyes, Mark.' With an enormous effort he forced himself to obey the voice, seeing a room spin round, as though viewed from a circling aeroplane, seeing a blurred face harden into perspective, feeling consciousness come back.

'That's it. That's right, my dear.' Tania's arm was under his head and her eyes were full of concern. 'And I'm so sorry, Mark, so terribly sorry. There was a door behind that curtain, you see, and . . .'

'Yes, I remember. He came through it when I opened the relic.' Against the hammer blows he recalled Karl Arnim's face rushing towards him and a bar swinging out to beat him down.

'Yes, and it was all my fault, Mark. Petrov told me to look after you and I never saw him till it was too late. He knocked the gun away from me before I could use it and then hit you with that length of pipe.'

'He certainly did.' Marcus felt the lump on his head and pulled himself to his feet. 'And after that he went out, I suppose, locking the door behind him?

'Let me have a look, though.' He lifted Tania's wrist. It was swollen and discoloured and bent at an odd angle. 'Yes, he gave you quite a knock too. You've got what is called a Colles fracture – a break at the lower end of the radius.' He smiled as he tore a strip from the altar cloth to make a bandage. 'I shall be becoming quite a wrist specialist before long. But did he say anything before he left?'

'Later, but I'm not sure what happened at the beginning because I passed out for a few minutes myself. When I came round, there was no sign of Arnim and I was only concerned about you. I thought you were dead, Mark . . . Then I saw Arnim again. There must be a room through there and he came out of it.' She pointed past the altar. The curtain had been pulled aside to show a board wall and a door fastened by a padlock. 'After he'd locked the door, he stood there for quite a time, leaning against the wall with his hand pressed on his cheek. I don't think he even knew we were there. He kept muttering to himself about his mother: how she had destroyed him years ago and was going to betray him now. I think he was weeping, but in this light I couldn't really be sure. He's crazy though, Mark; quite crazy.'

'Yes, he's crazy enough. Easy though.' He felt her shudder as he pulled the bandage tight and tied it. 'Crazy, or perhaps possessed would be the better word.' He turned and looked at the thing on the altar. In the dim light its withered skin looked like slag, and the ruby eyes might have been smiling at them. There was no question of what had happened now. As an amateur scientist Karl Arnim would have examined the tissue to see what preserving process had been used. And, as he laid a sliver of long-dead flesh on the microscope the moisture of his breath might have touched it. Then, when a stain had been added, he would have known that the spores were still alive.

'And then what happened, Tania?'

'He suddenly seemed to realize we were there. He had my gun in his right hand but he kept his left pressed against his cheek. He pointed the gun at me for a moment and then he shook his head and pushed it into his pocket. He went across to that thing on the altar and sort of bowed in front of it; genuflected I think the word is. He really was weeping as he passed me.'

'And then he went out?'

'Yes, by the door up into the church. He pulled it open and then he turned and looked back at us. As he did so, he uncovered his cheek and I could see that it was bleeding. Then he said . . . He spoke very quickly and I couldn't quite make it out. I think it was . . . "There's gratitude for you. I gave them freedom and one of the little blighters went and bit me." '

'He said that, did he?' Marcus ripped the rest of the curtain from the wall behind the altar. The boards were very flimsy and here and there they were uneven, leaving gaps above the floor.

' "I gave them freedom." The bastard! The crazy, bloody bastard.' He hurled himself at the door to the church, tugging at the handle and battering against the iron panels with his shoulder. He might just as well have tried to force his way into the vault of a bank. The lock and hinges were set in mortar and they didn't give a fraction of an inch. He leaned against it, gasping for breath and then turned and walked slowly back to the boarded wall. He pressed his ear against it, fighting to control the sound of his own heartbeats, and as he listened the pain in his forehead faded into complete unimportance. He'd felt fear many times in his life but never as badly as he did now, listening to the noises behind the boards. Tiny pattering, scraping noises that could have been made by sandpaper running over rough timber or light rain falling on grass. Time rolled back and he was standing in his room in the Central Laboratories watching the infected rats and noting his observations on a pad. 'For seven hours after infection, no apparent change in the animal was observed, but this was followed by a three-hour period of intense physical activity, aggression and the urge to escape.'

'He said that, my dear? "I gave them freedom." ' He walked across to Tania and suddenly pulled her to him, feeling a great strength and comfort from the touch of her body. He'd always imagined that he'd been through the worst terrors that life could offer, but now he knew he was quite wrong. The things behind that wall were unspeakable and, even as he listened, their noise was increasing. Scaly feet pattering on a stone floor, yellow teeth tearing at woodwork with now and again a scream or a shriek to punctuate them; a miasma, a sickness of the soil, a visitation from the stars to trouble the earth and drive the animals up into the world of men. The lamplight flickered on the thing upon the altar and its brass face seemed to be set in a wide smile of triumph.

'Yes,' he said, pulling Tania still closer to him. ' "I gave them freedom and one of the little blighters went and bit me." '

★   ★   ★

Gregor Petrov smelt strongly of lilies of the valley, but at least his car was warm. Kirk leaned comfortably back against the blast of an enormous rear heater and smiled approvingly as the drab suburbs of East Berlin slid past them.

Yes, things were going to be all right now. He was back on the job he understood, he was earning his keep, and everything was working out; though the last report of the epidemic was the worst yet. Everywhere stocks of vaccine were running low, cases were being reported from as far afield as Paris, and in London police had been brought from the provinces to control the crowds. Through the car window Kirk could see a long line of tense faces queueing in the snow before an inoculation centre. None of it worried him at all. His idea about the Morse code had worked, Gustav Behr had talked, and he and Petrov were both back on the job which they thoroughly understood.

Yes, *à chacun son métier*, every man to his trade. The saying ran pleasantly through Kirk's head against the whine of the engine. He had felt horribly useless until a few minutes ago, but now he was in charge again and everything would work out. Behr had talked, Levin's hunch had been proved correct and they knew all about the Fenwick child's movements. Clever Gretel's name was Gretel Arnim, or von Arnim, and she had been a key figure in the escape organization for years. Her contact in East Berlin was a man called Adolph Wolner, and on the day after Billy Fenwick disappeared Wolner had gone to Rudisheim to fetch him. That was all that Behr had told them before he died, but it was enough. Already the police were looking for Wolner, and he and Petrov were on their way to pay a call on Clever Gretel. It was a nuisance that they should have to go personally, but under the circumstances it had seemed necessary. The important thing was that he was back at his own job and doing something useful. He looked across at Petrov and, as though reading each other's thoughts, they both grinned.

'We have quite a long journey before us, my friend. I wonder if we could pass the time pleasantly.' Petrov pulled a small flat case from his pocket. 'This is one of my hobbies and I think I have heard that it is one of yours too.' He opened the case and the chessmen glinted as the car passed an illuminated sign reading 'Workers' Front Against War'.

'Would you like to give me a game?'

'Very much.' Kirk smiled back at him. 'I just hope that I'm good enough to play with a Russian.'

'Ah, yes, it is our national vice, isn't it? All the same, I'm just an amateur Russian.' He picked up two pawns and shuffled them in his hands.

'And to make things more interesting shall we have a bet on the result? The details of your decoding computer against the name of a certain British physicist who is intending to defect to us at a very early date? . . . no, of course not; that is merely a joke. Chess is too serious a business to mix with such trivialities.'

He held out his clenched fists and shook his head sadly as Kirk touched the left and revealed a red pawn.

'Ah, a pity. That should have been my colour, shouldn't it?' He switched on the roof light and laid the board on the seat between them.

'Now, how shall we start? Yes, you began your military career in the cavalry, so I'll meet you on your own ground.' The Russian smiled as he lifted his queen's knight and then they both stopped smiling. Only the game mattered to them now and neither of their old crafty minds would think of anything else till one of them nodded and acknowledged checkmate.

* * *

He was going to die and his death would be horrible, but so what? Karl Arnim laughed as he climbed into Tania's car. He deserved a horrible death, the whole of humanity did, and he would go out like a bomb; like a conqueror with an army of corpses around his funeral pyre.

Yes, here were the leads. The fools had removed the ignition key but it wouldn't take him long to make a connection. 'So what – so what – so what?' He hummed as his fingers tore the wires from the switch and started to twist them together.

A bomb – a great big bomb which he wouldn't waste in the bare fields of Rudisheim. It was going to explode where it could really do damage: amongst the busy streets of West Berlin, where the crowds poured out of the underground stations all day and family parties sat in the cafés on the Kurfürstendamm. That was the place where his bomb would be planted. 'Pardon, gn'e Frau, did I breathe on you?' 'Excuse me, please, sir. It is an unfortunate physical weakness. I spit slightly when I talk.'

'Dogs, would you live for ever?' Frederick the Great had asked his soldiers. Well, nobody was going to live long now. Not much longer than Marcus Levin and the Russian girl would live once the rats tore through that barrier.

And how much longer had he himself, if it came to that? Ten hours – twelve, perhaps? The tear in his cheek had stopped bleeding and was really hurting now. Already he could feel the stuff in his bloodstream, poisoning it, killing him. All the same, ten hours gave him plenty of time to do what he had to do.

But it wasn't his fault. Nothing had ever been his fault. At the beginning he'd never wanted to be evil. It was just that all his life he had been let down. Mutti had promised him so much and none of it had ever come true. That he was to be a pastor like his father and grandfather. That he would take a medical degree. That he would live in honour. 'Lies, lies, lies.' He screamed the words as he pressed the starter switch and then smiled as the engine burst into a merry hum.

Mutti would be dead now of course. She'd said that she would kill herself after he'd told her what had happened, and that was one promise she wouldn't break. Silly Mutti. Silly evil Gretel von Arnim. He'd loved her so much, but she deserved to die. 'You and I, Karl. You and I, my darling; always together.' He could still hear her voice and feel her arms around him, while upstairs in the little, stuffy bedroom his father had lain coughing his life away. 'My son can do anything he likes. My son isn't bound by rules or prejudices.' She deserved to die a thousand times for that night alone.

And now she'd let him down again. Everybody always let him down. After Levin had gone she'd screamed and raved at him, told him that she had borne a monster and didn't want to go on living. Well, perhaps she was right, but she had made him what he was and then deserted him. For years her work with the escape organization had taken all her energies and driven them steadily apart. Though that would be useful to him now of course. He took out a roughly drawn map of the route and studied it under the dashboard light. An empty shop in Fruchstrasse with a false wall in the cellar hiding a corridor which came out in the disused railway tunnel that ran through to the British sector. The same route through which they had taken Billy Fenwick.

But damn Billy – damn him to hell! It was Billy who had destroyed everything. He'd offered to help at first; to take the boy to Otto at Helmstedt, but Mutti hadn't wanted that. It was as though she didn't trust him any more, and she'd seemed to go crazy over the child, fondling him, crooning over him. And then he had taken Billy down to the crypt and showed him the relic, and he had laughed as though he were looking at some amusing toy. It was at that moment that he had known what possession was; as though somebody else had reached out for the chloroform and held the child's shoulders against the cage of fleas. Somebody else had opened the visor when Billy came to and somebody else's voice had said, 'You like fairy stories? Then look at one. Come and look at Iron Hans who can destroy the world if we let him loose.'

It all seemed so long ago when it had happened. After the church was bombed he had gone out and hidden the relic; 'an interesting historical curiosity', as the guide books called it, which should be preserved. Then, one day, when he was polishing it, he had made out the lines of verse and realized how to open it. It took him less than a day to discover that the things which killed Rudolph von Ginter were still alive.

But he hadn't wanted to harm anyone. It was just the feel of ownership that he liked. The knowledge that it was there; that Karl Arnim, the failure, the park-keeper, the man who had committed a sin which would never be forgiven him, held something as powerful as an atomic bomb in his hands. And then that damned child laughed!

And would anybody ever find Marcus Levin and the Russian girl, he wondered? Probably not, because there wouldn't be anybody left alive to find them. The first strain, the original strain could be beaten, of course. It responded to normal Pasteurella immuniza-tion, and before long they were bound to find an antibiotic to kill it. But the second form, the strain he had perfected and strength-ened and given to the rats, nothing could touch that. 'Excuse me, sir. Is my breath rather offensive?' He chuckled as he considered how it would be. 'My body is rotting, because when I opened the cages one of the little blighters bit me.' He broke off and his eyes blurred with pain.

'Oh, I wish – I wish – I wish . . .' Karl slid the car into gear and took one last look back through the window. Trees obscured his view of the house, but he knew that it was there; cosy and warm and hellish. It always would be there, just like that, till death blot-ted out his memory.

'Oh, I wish – I wish that only once – just once in all my life – I had slept with a woman who was not my mother.' He released the clutch and drove off: a blight moving across the clean snow into the world of men.

Nineteen

Judging by the noise, there could be scores of them behind that wall, a hundred even and, while the period of activity lasted, the creatures would attack anything that came their way. All fear had been driven out by pain and sickness and they were mad. The smell of man would certainly increase their mania.

But how long was it since they had become infected? How long would the active period last? If only there was something they could climb on to, they might have a chance. Marcus piled the last of the books along the foot of the wall and as he did so the sound of tearing wood seemed to increase. They would be in darkness as well before long. Already one of the lamps had gone out and Tania had checked the others and found that the oil was low in all of them. Her torch battery was almost dead, too.

No, the altar and the bookcases were no good: flimsy structures knocked together out of thin laths which wouldn't support their weight. Besides, rats had no difficulty in climbing up timber.

'There must be a way out. There has to be.' Tania's fingers clutched his arm. 'Let's try the door again, Mark. If we both tried to lift it together . . .'

'No, that's no good.'

He shook his head as he looked at the rotten plank with which they had attempted to lever the door off its hinges. They might as well have used a match stick.

'What we've got to do is to hold them back for just a little longer. Probably only two hours or even less.' He tried to put a little confidence into his voice, but without knowing when Arnim had infected the animals he couldn't be sure of anything. All he was really certain about was what had happened at the end. After the radio broadcast and their visit – after his mother had got the truth out of him, Arnim must have known that the game was up and he would have gone down to destroy the evidence. As he was doing so, he would have heard them come in and one last final blow against life must have occurred automatically to his crazed mind. And, as he opened the cages, 'One of the little blighters bit me.'

'No, it won't be for long. The organism runs down after three hours. Besides, the police are bound to start looking for us when we don't report back.' Once again he struggled to put assurance into the lie. Goltz and Braun would probably have forgotten the whole business by now and be peacefully snoring away beside their Fraus.

But it was impossible. It just couldn't happen; not to him. Sudden anger and disbelief mingled with his fears. It couldn't happen. He was Marcus Levin. When his new thesis on the enterin virus was published he would be well in the running for a Nobel prize. If he were due to die before his time it would have happened earlier; in Poland, or Belsen, or with Rachel in the Vietnam jungle. It was impossible that he should go out now. He looked across at Tania and knew that there was another reason why he couldn't die.

'Mark, Mark, look there – in the corner.' Her voice suddenly rose to a scream and he saw one of the books move jerkily forward. He tore a lath from the altar, knocking over the relic as he did so, and hurled himself at it, beating down at the gap between the wall and the leather spine. Under the stick something screamed, twisted, writhed upwards and then crunched.

'That's one of them we won't have to worry about any more.' Even as he spoke he heard Tania cry out again, and another book started to jerk out. It was right at the far end of the wall, too far for him to reach, and with an almost reflex action he pulled the nearest lamp from its bracket and threw it at the book. The paraffin flared up in an orange line, but there wasn't much of it, and after a minute it dwindled to choking grey smoke.

'You've stopped them, Mark. You've really stopped them.' Tania swung her torch along the wall. 'Listen.' Apart from their breathing there was complete silence in the room.

'I've stopped them for a little while. They'll be back very soon. All the same, there's a chance for you now.' The glare of the paraffin had shown him a niche in the wall which had been hidden by shadow, and he crossed over to it. It was quite small, probably intended to hold a statue, but one person could just get into it and no rat would climb those four feet of brickwork.

'Try and get up in there, my dear.'

'And sit watching you die?' She shook her head. 'No, I'm sorry, Mark, but you can't ask me to do that. It will only hold one of us and I'm staying here with you.'

'Very well, if that's the way you want it.' He turned from the niche and came towards her, shrugging his shoulders. 'Thank you. And, Tania, if we get out of this, there's something I'd like you to remember. Though we've only known each other for a few hours, I think I'm in love with you.' He held out his left hand and, as their fingers touched, his right fist swung at her chin with all his strength behind it.

'Sorry about that, my sweet, but perhaps your husband will be grateful to me one day.' Marcus lifted her unconscious body into the niche. There was a rusty iron hook driven into the brickwork and he took off his tie and fastened her waist to it, grinning sadly as he pulled the tasteful device of crossed alpenstocks into a knot. He had been very proud when they asked him to join the Il Vagabondo Club. Its current membership included two Nobel Prize winners, a Catholic cardinal, a Cabinet minister, proposed on the strength of his book on Etruscan architecture, and the Archbishop of Canterbury, who had only got in by the skin of his teeth.

'Well, that's one of us taken care of.' He glanced at his right hand. There must have been a nail in the lath he had taken from the altar and blood was pouring from a deep cut in the palm. As he looked at it, a verse from Housman ran through his head. When he first came to England he had thought the people to be without emotion till he had started to read their poetry.

' "And here's a bloody hand to shake," ' he said aloud to the almost silent room. ' "And, oh, man, here's goodbye. We'll sweat no more on scythe or rake, my bloody hands and I.' "

And it would be goodbye soon. The last of the smoke had drifted away and the noise was starting again. It sounded quieter and more subdued at first and then steadily grew in volume as though the animals had been goaded into fresh activity by their setback. Beside him one of the three remaining lamps flickered and went out, and he seemed to hear a parody of the television slogan mocking him: 'Marcus Levin, this is your death.'

But there – over there. Marcus grabbed the lath as another book jerked away from the wall. The creature was already out of its prison, pulling itself up through a gnawed hole in the wood and glaring at him with red, tortured eyes. His stick lashed out, breaking its back, but there was another rat beside it and this one didn't pause. It leapt up at him in a bouncing arc, gripping the lath in its teeth and swinging from it like a bulldog. He dashed it to the floor, seeing it twist away to safety, knowing that there would be another one following it, and another, and another, but concentrating on nothing except killing the first. He never heard the noise behind him: feet running down the stairs, the door bursting open, and the shots. He never saw the beam of light. He just went on slashing at the rat till it turned and sprang at him. It was within inches of his throat when Gregor Petrov's third bullet killed it.

* * *

'Yes, we were quite literally here in the nick of time, Sir Marcus. In at the kill, eh?' Kirk beamed at him. 'It reminds me a bit of that H. G. Wells story, *The Food of the Gods*. You remember, when they hear the newspaper boys shouting "Doctor eaten by stupendous Rats."'

'Yes, I suppose it might remind one of that.' Marcus found the remark both tasteless and unfunny. It was two hours since he and Tania had been rescued and they had been partially restored by brandy at the local hotel. But now, as he stood at the top of the steps to the crypt again, nausea was coming back. 'If one had a particularly perverse sense of humour, that is.'

'Oh, sorry, old boy. Poor taste, eh?' Kirk sniffed the air and turned to the leader of the decontamination unit which had been sent over from Magdeburg. 'I suppose that it's safe enough to go in there?'

'Perfectly safe, Herr General.' The man clicked his heels and pronounced the title with a flourish. 'We pumped the place full of potassium cyanide, killing everything, but extractor fans have been at work and the air should be quite pure now.'

'Should be?' Petrov raised his eyebrows. 'It had better be, comrade, or I can picture a very miserable future for you and yours. Well, gentlemen, are you ready?'

'I suppose so.' In spite of the hint of a grin on Kirk's face, Marcus took Tania's arm as he went down the steps. High up in the vaulted ceiling of the crypt there was an electric bulb which they hadn't discovered, and in its glare he could see the relic lying on the floor, the lath that had saved his life and the dead bodies of the rats. They looked quite innocent now — just small bundles of brown and grey fur; nothing to do with the things that had slashed and screamed at him.

'Yes, Arnim made himself quite a business-like laboratory.' The door in the partition had been broken open to show the room behind it. More dead rats lay on the floor, there was a huge wire cage in the centre, and benches ran along the walls, piled with scientific equipment.

'He must have worked very hard, too.' There was admiration in Marcus's eyes as he looked at the apparatus. Apart from a modern microscope it was terribly crude and old-fashioned, and some of it appeared to have been homemade. He studied it briefly, and then opened a book at the end of the third bench: Arnim's notes.

'Yes, I see.' He flushed with excitement as he read the spidery writing. 'So, that's it. All the time, right under our noses and we never even bothered to try it. Histocyn 2.'

'What's that, old boy? You've found something important?'

'Yes, I think you can call it important, General.' Marcus nodded without looking up. 'There is a drug to kill the bacillus. According to Arnim it has no resistance to Histocyn.' He flicked on through the pages.

'There doesn't appear to be any doubt about it. He used all the standard tests and it was effective in every case. Once we can get production going, there'll be no need to worry about this little beauty any more.

'Have this sent out to all medical authorities at once, will you?' Marcus scribbled a note and handed it to Petrov. 'And don't think too badly that we didn't discover it ourselves. Histocyn 2 was one of the very early antibiotics, developed in Holland soon after the discovery of penicillin. It is thought to be effective only in dealing with certain localized complaints – sinus infections, for example – and rarely used these days. I suppose we would have tried it in time, but very much as a last resort.' He glanced at the dates on the book. 'After all, Arnim has been studying the bacillus for fifteen years.'

'Don't worry, Sir Marcus. Nobody will ever criticize you.' Petrov gave the note to one of the policemen. 'Your hunch about coming here paid off right along the line, and please accept my congratulations.' He mopped his forehead with a very bright silk handkerchief.

'So, everything will be back to normal again, it seems. This – this stuff of yours can stop the bug, and there'll be nothing more to worry about. You can go home, eh, General, and start getting to grips with my successor, and I can look forward to a long and well-earned retirement. Thank you.' Another policeman hurried into the room and Petrov took a message pad from him.

'Ah, good.' He smiled as he read. 'They've located this man, Adolph Wolner, who took the child through to West Berlin. For some reason, perhaps merely luck, he is not infected. He hasn't told us about the escape route yet, but there's no doubt that he will do after my boys have had a little time with him. And when he has talked we'll put an end to this escaping business once and for all.' Now that the crisis had passed Petrov was getting back to his routine problems.

'But Arnim? Any news of him yet?'

'No, not at the moment, but don't worry. We'll find him soon enough. A full description has gone out and road blocks have been set up. It's merely a question of time before Herr *von* Arnim, as he likes to call himself, is shot down like – how do you say – a mad dog.'

'Yes, mad enough, but a clever dog too.' Marcus read on through the notes and a pleasant picture was forming in his mind. A series of lectures, a new mention in the Honours List, his picture in every newspaper, a very rosy future indeed. He looked across at Tania and smiled. He was far too old for her and they would make an ill-assorted couple. Doubtless his housekeeper, Mrs Armstrong, who was a staunch Conservative, would be full of disapproval too. To hell with his age! To hell with Mrs Armstrong! She would just have to get used to the idea. He remembered how he had sung on the way to Richmond and almost started to hum the refrain. Then he turned another page and everything became cold again.

'No, no, please God, no. Let him have failed – please let him have failed.' The writing seemed to twist and blur in front of his eyes, but there it was. 'October 15th, 1961 . . . Today I commenced experiments to see if it is possible to produce a strain which will be resistant to the normal Pasteurella serum. Dr Runeberg who is indebted to my mother for his daughter's presence in the West has promised to obtain supplies of the serum for me . . .' Six pages of dates and figures, and at last three lines of cramped writing. 'I have done it. Now to see if immunity to Histocyn 2 can be produced. The key may well be through intense radiation. I will try ultra violet first.'

'Yes, that might be a possibility.' On the shelf over the bench Marcus could see an outlandish piece of equipment which resembled a magic lantern. It had battery carbons fitted as burning elements and the reflector had been taken from an electric fire. Though it looked a horribly botched and amateur job, he had no doubt that the power would be there. He stared at the notes again and he had never prayed harder in his life.

'Failure – failure.' Across every page, covering weeks and months and years, the word had been scribbled in red pencil, obscuring the notes. Marcus felt hope coming back as he looked at it. 'January – August – November – 1962 – '63 – '64. Failure – failure – failure.' Then, almost at the end of the book, dated less than a week ago, the entry that told him hope had died. 'It should now be perfect and I have enough subjects to make a thorough test.'

Yes, he had had enough all right. Marcus stood up and looked at the cage. It was divided into dozens of partitions, but they could all be opened by a single lever if necessary. Beside it was another small cage of very fine wire mesh with what looked like a pile of dust on the floor. Neither of them was of any importance now. Cyanide had killed the rats and the fleas and there was only one carrier left. Just as Arnim had released the rats, 'one of the little blighters bit me.'

'I'm sorry, gentlemen.' Marcus turned to Kirk and Petrov. 'I thought we were home at last, but I was wrong – quite wrong.' The mere effort of speech was almost too much for him. 'Arnim produced a mutant, you see; a species which is unaffected by the Pasteurella serum and also resistant to Histocyn. He is infected with it himself.'

'Only himself? Only Arnim?' Petrov smiled reassuringly. 'Then don't worry, Sir Marcus. The police have his description and . . .'

'And they will shoot him down like a mad dog, as you said before.'

Marcus shook his head and tried to imagine what might happen. If they merely wounded Arnim and he staggered away into a crowd of onlookers. If a bullet grazed him and went on to find another target, carrying a smear of his poisoned blood with it. If a police dog sniffed his breath before he died.

'You'll have to change your instructions to the police, I'm afraid, Mr Petrov. Arnim is a carrier and his one ambition will be to pass on the disease to others. That is normal enough with the sane, and he's a psychopath. Samuel Pepys reported that during the Plague of London, "Ill people would breathe in the faces of well people passing by."

'No, tell your police not to interfere with Arnim till they've got him where they can't miss – where there's not the slightest chance of his escaping. It's not a question of *killing* Arnim any more. He must be completely destroyed.'

Twenty

It was almost as though they had been avoiding him. As though they knew what he could do to them and were keeping out of his way; avoiding him like the plague. Karl Arnim grinned, partly at the thought and partly to stifle pain; clenching his teeth to try and control the shudders which were running through his body.

Yes, almost as though they knew. It was just after Magdeburg when he had come across the first road block. Two police cars drawn up on the verge and their occupants standing in the road with machine pistols under their arms. He was sure that they would try to stop him and he had prepared to make a dash for it, but one of them had waved him on. And, after all, why should they stop him? Nobody could say that he wasn't a perfectly respectable citizen. Not

Mutti, nor Marcus Levin nor the Russian girl. Nobody could accuse him of anything.

All the same, he'd been careful after that, turning off into minor roads and approaching the city from the south-east. At Friedrichhain he had left the car in a side street, because private vehicles were likely to attract attention in central Berlin and also because he wanted to walk; to feel clean air in his lungs and the snow, which was beginning to fall again, cool against his burning face.

It was soon after that that he'd had his second encounter with the police. Three of them, a sergeant and two very young constables had come slowly towards him down the pavement. He had been almost on the point of running, but the sergeant had said something to his companions and they'd all walked across the road; again as though they knew.

And perhaps they did. Perhaps some sixth sense in their stupid, animal minds told them to beware of him. It was pleasant to think that, and also pleasant to think of them dying, rotting; just as he himself was beginning to rot. In a strange way he almost felt offended that they had not tried to stop him.

After the police had come the drunks. Five horrible, 'for tomorrow we die' drunks lurching along in the centre of the road. One of the men had paused to vomit in the gutter and the two women were howling out a bawdy song. Though it was bitterly cold he could see that one of them had her blouse ripped open, showing a glint of bare flesh.

Yes, 'for tomorrow we die' was right and he loved them, because they were behaving exactly as the human animal was supposed to behave. In the Middle Ages sexual activity had been considered a protection against plague, and these drunks were following the pattern. He would have liked to go up to them, raise his arm to quiet the bawling hags and shout, 'Bless you, my creatures. I made you what you are.'

Then had come the immunization centre near the Ostbahnhof. A long queue standing in the snow and shuffling forward. It was quite an orderly queue, because there was a squad of police watching them, but the strain on every face was clear enough in spite of the reassurances which poured out from a loudspeaker. 'There is no cause for alarm – the only danger is panic – ample stocks of vaccine are being flown in from the Soviet Union – it is just a matter of time before the epidemic is under full control.'

That was true enough. Karl nodded in agreement as he listened. Soon there would be no danger at all. The vaccine would take and before long somebody like Marcus Levin would hit on Histocyn and the strain would be wiped out. Only the original strain, though. It would take a long, long time to get the measure of the second creature – the one which he had strengthened and perfected and which was coursing through his bloodstream now. Once again he had a desire to go up to them, to tell them who he was, but he fought against it and walked on. It wasn't among these small pathetic groups that his blow would fall, but among the jostling, hurrying crowds of the West.

But here he was at last: Fruchstrasse, a narrow, dingy street with half the buildings unoccupied and the scars of bombing still plainly visible. The shop he wanted was on the next corner with a sign reading 'Glass and Novelties' on the fascia.

Before the wall went up, it must have sold ornamental ash-trays, and tiny glass animals, and beer mugs which played a tune when they were lifted from the table. Now it had been shut for years and only people who knew its secret would visit it. On the boards across the window there was a poster advertising some athletic meeting at the Volkspark; two tall, bronzed girls leaping across hurdles. Karl stared at them for a moment and then glanced up and down the street. He was quite alone and there was no need to hurry. Six o'clock of a fine clear morning, the snow blowing away and a hint of dawn coming up in the east. Between eight and nine was the time he wanted. Then the crowds would be flooding the underground stations and he would be with them. He moved to the door and then paused and stared up at the poster as though his eyes were being pulled towards it.

'Oh, I wish,' he said to the empty street, and the cold air, and the faded, torn paper, 'oh, I wish that just once, I could have known somebody like one of you.' He pushed open the door and walked forward to his destiny.

*   *   *

The car radio had been choked with static since they left Rudisheim and now the loudspeaker was almost useless. The operator
sat hunched beside the driver with earphones on and he scribbled
what he could make out on a pad, handing back each message to
Petrov. As he read the last one the Russian frowned and shook his
head.

'Well, I just hope we're doing the right thing, General,' he said.
'As you know, Arnim reached the road block outside Lenzfeld
shortly after three and, according to instructions, no attempt was
made to stop him. We now know that he left the car in Friedrichhain and is going west on foot.' He scowled at Tania. 'Though you
were in a hurry, surely you could have remembered to lock the car
door?'

'It was I who left the door unlocked, Mr Petrov, and it's a good
thing I did. If Arnim had gone by public transport or tried to get a
lift, there would be the very devil to pay.'

'Yes, I suppose you're right.' Petrov grinned at Marcus. 'But
what an attractive phrase, "the very devil to pay". I must try to remember that.

'At any rate, from what we learned from his mother, it seems
certain that Arnim is making for West Berlin. As soon as Wolner
tells us about the route, we shall bring up the equipment General
Kirk so wisely suggested and there will be nothing to worry about.'
He pulled out a case and offered cigarettes all round; the courteous
host attending to his guests' comfort.

'And perhaps this will be what we are waiting for.' He pushed
away his lighter as the operator handed him another note. 'Yes,
Wolner has talked all right. I thought he would after my boys had
a little time with him.

'It seems that in the Fruchstrasse there is a shop with a concealed
door in its cellar. Behind this, a passage has been dug through to
one of the main sewers, and the route finally comes out in the underground railway system. Since we stopped traffic, all inter-city
lines are blocked of course, but they have cut an opening in one
of the barriers. But . . .' Petrov broke off. He had been smiling as

he read, but now he suddenly looked very worried. He handed the paper to Kirk.

'And that's all we do know, General; all that Wolner was able to tell them. For obvious reasons he was only given part of the route.'

'Thank you. Yes, natural enough, I suppose, but it puts us on the spot.' Kirk's maimed hand trembled on the arm rest as he spoke. 'In case he should be caught, Wolner was only given details of the route as far as the railway block. From there on the escapers were escorted by an agent from the west: this woman Ruth Eulenburg, who is dead.' He picked up a map of Berlin and scowled at its mass of railway lines.

'So, I'll have to send the police in after him.' Petrov hated the thought of that, for he could picture a squad of men blundering through the tunnels. The chances were that they wouldn't even find Arnim, but if they did – if he turned on them before a lethal bullet went home . . .

'You may have to do so, if he has already reached the shop, but I don't like the idea at all. As Sir Marcus says, we want him out in the open where he can't be missed.' Kirk bent over the map, trying to put himself in Arnim's place and understand the workings of his crazed mind. Once he was through the barrier separating east from west, he could go where he liked, but he must have some specific destination. He leaned forward to the radio operator.

'You are a Berliner?' he said holding the map out to him. 'Good. Now, this railway is called the "U-bahn" or "Untergrundbahn", but it is really a simple cut-and-cover system which often runs on the surface. Can you indicate which are surface lines in this section here?

'Thank you.' He nodded as the man drew a series of crosses on the map. 'Now, I'd like you to try and contact British Military Headquarters in Charlottenburg. The wavelength is fifteen point five metres and the code words to get them to answer are "Wuthering Heights".' He leaned back on his seat and held the map out in front of him. If he had read Arnim's mind correctly, the man would remain underground till the last possible moment and he would want to make his appearance at a big station. That ruled out the line between the Leipzigerplatz and Yorkstrasse, and also from

Friedrichstrasse to the Lehterbahnhof. There was just one obvious choice. He drew a circle around a station and handed the map to Petrov.

'Yes, I think it's going to be up to our people to deal with Arnim now and, unless I'm completely wrong, this is where they should wait for him.' Kirk closed his eyes for a moment as the operator struggled to make the connection he needed. He had made his last move and played his hunch as Marcus Levin had done and, once he had given his orders, there would be nothing more for him to do. He considered the crowds which would soon be filling the underground system and he prayed he was right.

'And, if I'm wrong,' he said, partly to himself and partly to his companions, 'if I'm wrong, God help us.'

* * *

Seven forty-five. The little luminous dial of his watch told him that it was time to go, and Karl hoped that it wasn't much farther. His body was hardly capable of obeying him now and his feet stumbled and dragged on the floor of the disused tunnel.

Yes, he'd have to take it very slowly, because he was almost finished. It was like an eternity since he had entered that shop in the Fruchstrasse, crawling on his knees down the narrow corridor and wading through foul water as he crossed the sewer. But at last his torch had found the grating and he had pulled himself up into the railway tunnel.

It was shortly after that that the police had come. Three of them marching officiously up to the brick barrier as he crouched behind a pillar. It had obviously been a routine patrol, because they had merely swung a lamp over it and clumped off as though satisfied. Fools! Incompetent fools! If they had only looked a little closer they must have seen the tiny line of metal in the brickwork. The door which when pushed in a certain manner swung back to show the way to the west.

Clever Gretel. Clever, clever Gretel von Arnim. She'd destroyed him. The sin they had committed together might make his soul rot in hell, just as his body was rotting now, but he had felt enormous admiration for her as he crawled through the door that she and her associates had made. Clever, clever Gretel.

He must be almost there now. The rusty nails between his feet started to throb and hum and, less than a hundred yards away, he could see a string of lights as a train clattered across a junction. He held the torch over his map. The refugee lines had to be kept secret, even in the west, and at this point there should be an air shaft with a loose cover that led up to a piece of waste ground behind the station. To hell with the refugees, to hell with crawling up air shafts, even if he had the strength to do so. It was the station itself and the early morning crowds that he wanted. Very serious crowds probably. Worried people thinking about the epidemic, but still secure in the knowledge that 'it can't happen to me'. It was going to happen though. He grinned at the thought of them standing there, with their newspapers like barriers before them. Then one of them would turn and see him climb up on to the barrier and . . . There was a nursery rhyme that Miss Steele, his English governess, had taught him. 'Atishooo – atishoo – we all fall down.'

Karl threw the map and the torch away and staggered forward. His throat appeared to be furred up and now and again he had to lean against the wall, gasping for breath. That's right, he thought. Not far now, so take it nice and slow and easy. Mind that pillar and look out for trains at the junction. Such a very little way to go, and you must make it because they are waiting for your entrance, for the grand performance. The rusty nails joined others which were shiny with use and he could see the station.

Yes, there it was, though his lungs were bursting with the effort, and at every step he could feel the thing in his groin grate and swell. Such a little way. Fifty metres, thirty, twenty, there. The platform reared up like a cliff, but his arms grasped the top and he pulled himself up till he was kneeling on the edge, seeing nothing but a red glow at first and then slowly opening his eyes and looking at the world he had come to destroy.

But no, it wasn't true. It couldn't be true. It was just his eyes deceiving him – the poison in his body distorting sight. He stared along the platform, seeing confectionery and cigarette machines, advertisements and signs reading 'Kurfürstenplatz' along the walls and a clock showing seven minutes past eight. But nobody was there; nobody at all. Arnim shook his head in bewilderment, and then smiled.

For that was it, of course. Somewhere along the route he had made a mistake and come out at the wrong station. A station which was out of use because it only connected with the east and the lines were blocked. The name signs were just a trick of the eyes; wish fulfilment brought on by disease. Somewhere he had missed the turning, but it wasn't important. He only had to get out into the daylight, into the fresh air, and he would find people to accept his legacy. 'Excuse me, sir, I'm afraid that I spit slightly when I speak. It is a weakness.'

With a gasping, shambling effort Karl moved on. He crawled up the steps to the booking office on his knees; more deserted machines, no porter at the barrier, no woman in the newspaper stand and more signs mocking him; 'Kurfürstenplatz' – an illusion. But, at last, he saw a passage with daylight at the end of it.

It was a lovely day too. 'A lovely day to die on,' as the French queen had said on her way to the guillotine. Under an almost cloudless sky the snow-covered buildings looked like Christmas cakes. Their cakes – his and Mutti's cakes – Gretel von Arnim's cakes to be consumed with love while the chestnuts popped on the stove and everything was warm and cosy.

And there were the police waiting to welcome him. Dozens of them standing at the other side of the street with a little group of soldiers in front of them. British soldiers – Tommies. The same khaki soldiers who had given him his wound. They carried no guns, but one of them had two cylinders strapped to his back and held what looked like a length of hose-pipe in his right hand. The sergeant at his side wore a row of campaign ribbons on his tunic and there was a blue cockade in his cap which showed that he belonged to a crack regiment.

Well, a British soldier would be the first victim. Karl stood grinning at them from the station entrance and then broke into a stumbling run. 'Here I come, Sergeant,' he thought. 'Here I come with my present.' He stopped as a car came into the square and drew up beside the soldiers. Four people got out. Two old men in very thick overcoats with faces that looked strangely alike, and after them ghosts – the dead – Marcus Levin and the Russian girl, coming to see his end. Behind him Karl heard the station gates crash together, cutting off his escape, and he suddenly realized what the cylinders meant.

'No,' he screamed. 'No, no, no, don't shoot. Friend, Ami, Kamerad, please don't shoot! I don't mean any harm! I just want to give you something!' He went on screaming like that till one of the old men gave an order, the soldier lifted the nozzle of his flame-thrower and pulled the trigger.

RECENT AND FORTHCOMING TITLES FROM VALANCOURT BOOKS

Michael Arlen	Hell! said the Duchess
R. C. Ashby	He Arrived at Dusk
Frank Baker	The Birds
Charles Beaumont	The Hunger and Other Stories
Charles Birkin	The Smell of Evil
John Blackburn	A Scent of New-Mown Hay
	Broken Boy
	Blue Octavo
	A Ring of Roses
	Children of the Night
	The Flame and the Wind
	Nothing but the Night
	Bury Him Darkly
	Our Lady of Pain
	Devil Daddy
	The Household Traitors
	The Face of the Lion
	The Cyclops Goblet
	A Beastly Business
	The Bad Penny
Thomas Blackburn	A Clip of Steel
	The Feast of the Wolf
Michael Blumlein	The Brains of Rats
Basil Copper	The Great White Space
	Necropolis
	The House of the Wolf
A. E. Ellis	The Rack
Barry England	Figures in a Landscape
Ronald Fraser	Flower Phantoms
Michael Frayn	Sweet Dreams
Stephen Gilbert	The Landslide
	Monkeyface
	The Burnaby Experiments
	Ratman's Notebooks
Stephen Gregory	The Cormorant
	The Woodwitch
	The Blood of Angels
Alex Hamilton	Beam of Malice
Thomas Hinde	The Day the Call Came

Claude Houghton	I Am Jonathan Scrivener
	This Was Ivor Trent
Fred Hoyle	The Black Cloud
Gerald Kersh	Fowlers End
	Nightshade and Damnations
Hilda Lewis	The Witch and the Priest
John Lodwick	Brother Death
Michael McDowell	The Amulet
	Cold Moon Over Babylon
	The Elementals
Oliver Onions	The Hand of Kornelius Voyt
J.B. Priestley	Benighted
	The Doomsday Men
	The Other Place
	The Magicians
	Saturn Over the Water
	The Shapes of Sleep
	The Thirty-First of June
	Salt Is Leaving
Piers Paul Read	Monk Dawson
Forrest Reid	Brian Westby
	Denis Bracknel
Andrew Sinclair	The Raker
	Gog
	The Facts in the Case of E. A. Poe
David Storey	Radcliffe
	Pasmore
	Saville
Russell Thorndike	The Slype
	The Master of the Macabre
John Wain	Hurry on Down
	The Smaller Sky
	A Winter in the Hills
Hugh Walpole	The Killer and the Slain
Keith Waterhouse	There is a Happy Land
	Billy Liar
	Jubb
	Billy Liar on the Moon
Colin Wilson	Ritual in the Dark
	Man Without a Shadow
	Necessary Doubt
	The Glass Cage
	The Philosopher's Stone
	The God of the Labyrinth

www.ingramcontent.com/pod-product-compliance
Lightning Source LLC
Chambersburg PA
CBHW011750010726
47498CB00012B/3002